Praise

"The ebb and flow of love and life, and the minute details that make us human are revealed though Annalisa Crawford's deceptively simple writing . Funny, sassy stories, laced with yearning and affection, these are intimate pieces that will resonate. A lovely collection."
RAFFAELLA BARKER, AUTHOR OF *A PERFECT LIFE*

"Crawford has an extraordinary ability to create fully-formed characters we care about in just a few words. We are horrified by some of the characters, such as a spirit trapped in a house she can't leave, and enchanted by others, including an elderly couple still in love after 60 years of marriage. This is a beautiful collection of stories guaranteed to touch readers and stay with them long after they have read the last page."
JULIE FLANDERS, AUTHOR OF *POLAR NIGHT* & *POLAR DAY*

"With subtle nuance, Crawford's stories pierce the essence of life, love, and character. Dreams vs. reality. Work vs. fun. Sketches filled with love, yearning, and disappointment. Annalisa Crawford captures life in this timeless collection. Rich writing and heartbreaking depth of emotion strike at the soul in Crawford's *You. I. Us.*"
JOANNE FARIES, AUTHOR OF *WORDSPLASH FLASH*

D1452934

About the Author

Annalisa Crawford lives in Cornwall UK, with a good supply of moorland and beaches to keep her inspired. She lives with her husband, two sons, a dog and a cat. Annalisa writes dark contemporary, character-driven stories. She has been winning competitions and publishing short stories in small press journals for many years, and is the author of *Cat & The Dreamer* and *Our Beautiful Child*.

Visit Annalisa: *www.annalisacrawford.com*

You. I. Us.
Copyright © 2016 Annalisa Crawford
All rights reserved.

Print Edition
ISBN: 978-1-925417-17-3
Published by Vine Leaves Press 2016
Melbourne, Victoria, Australia

This is a work of fiction. Any similarity between the characters and situations within its pages and places or persons, living or dead, is unintentional and coincidental.

Cover design by Jessica Bell
Interior design by Amie McCracken

National Library of Australia Cataloguing-in-Publication entry (pbk)
Author: Crawford, Annalisa, author
Title: You. I. Us. / Annalisa Crawford.
ISBN: 9781925417173 (paperback)
Subjects: Short stories.
Emotions--Fiction.
Choice (Psychology)--Fiction.
Dewey Number: 823.92

you. i. us.

Annalisa Crawford

Regards
[signature]

Vine Leaves Press
Melbourne, Vic, Australia

Table of Contents

For my boys, Connor and Ollie.

My Song

You wrote a song for me.

I didn't give you anything in return. Not even myself.

You unveiled it in the bustling sixth form common room; you'd borrowed a mate's keyboard and waited impatiently for me to get out of double English. So sure it would work—that I'd fall into your arms and declare undying love—you never gave a thought to the piss-taking you'd have to endure afterwards. Your mates were merciless for weeks.

You sang, and I listened. It was okay, good; although somewhat bizarre to know the song was about me. I remember cringing when you mentioned my sexy shoulders, and tried to rhyme it with *closer*.

You looked at me when you finished, and I wasn't sure what to do next, whether I should thank you, or applaud … or tell you that I wasn't interested, no matter how many songs you wrote for me. But, I was seventeen. I blushed furiously, mumbled incoherently, and allowed myself to be pulled away by my sniggering friends.

When I looked back, you'd disappeared.

I'm holding the song in my hand now, staring at your messy scrawled writing, at all the words you crossed out in favour of another, like *searching* instead of *looking*, *scorching hearts* in place of *bright stars*. You'd doodled a border of musical notes and smiley faces and hearts. There's a coffee stain across the bottom of the page, and I'm not sure if you caused that while you were composing late into the night, or if I did it, carelessly, later.

The paper is crispy with age, the edges have browned. It's more than ten years old, after all. I stare at the words again, and remember the sound of your voice. You always had a good voice.

I'm surprised I kept the song, to be honest. I don't remember doing it on purpose—more likely I just overlooked throwing it out.

No one really knew what happened to you, after A Levels. It was like you vanished.

And here you are, on my telly, right now. I scrutinize the screen, to make absolutely sure it's you. I reach for my mobile, ready to announce it on Facebook, but I don't. I don't think I want to share this with anyone.

You're being interviewed by two excitable presenters; they're introducing you as the *next big thing* before you take your place on the John Peel stage. Apparently, you got famous and you're playing *Glastonbury!* No one expected that.

People cheer as you leave the interview area and walk out onto the stage. Teenage girls scream your name and wave banners as they sing along with your debut number one song. They already know all the words. There are kids in that crowd who want to be *you*, the way you wanted to be Damien Rice. It's pretty surreal.

"The next song," you say, catching your breath and waiting for the whooping to subside, "was written a long time ago, for someone special."

You look deep into the camera, as though you know I'm watching. I realize I'm sitting on the edge of my chair, holding my breath. You sing my song, like you did all those years ago, and I sing along.

Motherhood

I

I'm sorry, so sorry.

You're wired up, your tiny heart beating through tissue-paper skin. You're far too small—your hand doesn't even wrap itself around one of my fingers.

It's my fault.

Yesterday safe, protected and warm, you snuggled securely within my womb. You sucked your thumb, the way you did in your scan photos. You kicked out in time with the bongs at the start of the news, your little foot pressing itself against my stomach so I could see the faint outline.

I don't know what happened. I went to bed last night after a warm bath, looking forward to the holiday Daddy was going to take me on—a last-minute trip to Ghent before you arrived. Daddy lay down next to me, his head resting against you, and we talked while you repeatedly punched him in the face. When my eyes got heavy, he kissed my forehead, kissed my stomach—kissed *you*—and went downstairs.

But I was restless. I had a bad dream. My grandmother, your great-grandmother, was in the corner of the room, hiding in the shadows so I couldn't quite see her. She was trying to tell me something, but I couldn't hear her. I kept asking her to repeat herself, but she didn't, or couldn't.

Then she began fading into the walls, into the darkness. I tried to run towards her, but the sheets pinned me down. I fought against them, calling out for help. They got tighter, squeezing until I couldn't breathe.

When I woke, the contractions had already started, far too

early. Daddy told me it was going to be all right—he said it was just a mistake and you wouldn't be going anywhere for a long time yet.

He was wrong. Here you are.

This isn't how I imagined the first few days of your life. We should be elated. I should be holding you, nursing you, kissing your beautiful face. I couldn't wait to show you off to my friends, and introduce you to your new family. They'd all want to hold you too, and we'd take so many photos. Daddy would buy you a giant teddy bear, and he'd buy me a bouquet of flowers. We made plans; we had your life all mapped out.

But here I am, sitting in a small room while noisy equipment keeps you alive. The lights are low, so they don't hurt your eyes, and the nurses whisper so they don't disturb me. They make no sound when they walk.

Daddy went home to rest, and to phone your nanny and granddad. They'll want to come and see you, of course, but I don't think they'll be allowed. It's just you and me, you lovely little lady.

I have my hand resting inside the incubator, my finger stroking your cheek. My hand is bigger than your torso. Your heart pumps rapidly, trying its very best. Your arms and legs are spread out. I haven't heard you cry yet; I haven't seen your eyes.

I'm waiting.

II

You cry, no matter how much I rock you, no matter how much I jiggle you up and down. In the end, before I tear my hair out or burst into exhausted tears, I put you in your pram and we leave the house.

I have nothing to do, no errands to run, so I wander aimlessly for a while. I could go to a café, I suppose, but you're bound to fuss if we stop moving. And besides, this pram is huge. I cause chaos wherever I go.

Or I could call on a friend, except they'll all be at work at this time on a Tuesday morning. I joined a mother's group for a while—the health visitor suggested it—but I hated the way everyone stared at you. I wanted to hide you away, shield you.

It's obvious there's something different about you, although it takes people a moment to figure it out. Which means they stare longer than I'm comfortable with. The initial reactions are the worst, the unguarded ones, before they've had time to catch themselves. Your early arrival caused brain damage, although the extent will be unknown until you start to develop, or *not* develop, the doctor said.

You don't focus properly, and your vacant expression gives you the appearance of being mildly confused by everything. Of course, the giveaway—the moment people retreat, with a sympathetic smile—is the shape of your head, a bit squished, discoloured with the remnants of bruising. It's only been three and a half months—your poor body is still recovering from the trauma.

You like being out in the fresh air. Your little arms beat against the sides of the pram. You have a smile—at least, something that I call a smile—on your face. We pass the park gates, and I turn in. Why not? There's a pond there, and you like to look at the ducks. I expect we'll spend a lot of time here once you start walking.

I nod politely to the grey-haired lady feeding the ducks. "Hello."

"Hello, dear." She stands upright and peeks down at you.

I tense.

She reaches out and pats your hand.

"Well, hello there," she coos, with a genuine smile. "She's adorable. How old?"

"Fourteen weeks."

"What's her name?"

"Cassie."

"Oh, how lovely."

I sigh and rock the pram. You're wriggling around, kicking your legs against the blanket. You wail softly. You always sound as if you're in pain, and I sometimes can't bear it. I can't do anything to help, and yet it's all my fault. If I was alone, I'd be weeping now; not sobbing, but I'd definitely be walking along with tears rolling down my face, too drained to wipe them away.

"It's not an easy age, is it? All those sleepless nights." She's still tickling your cheek. You watch her intently.

"No, especially with this one. She needs so much care. It doesn't stop." I gaze down at you for a moment. You need so much from me, I don't think I can be enough. I'm aware of the lady watching me. "Well," I say, overly jolly, "I must get on, almost time for her feed."

"It was nice to meet you both. I'm always here, at this time, if you and Cassie want to help me feed the ducks."

I smile and nod, unable to stop a couple of tears welling up. Such simple words, such a huge impact.

III

The gates are intimidating, foreboding. They loom down on us, heavy and dark, solid so that we can't see beyond them.

I can only imagine how they must appear to you. Your eyes start at ground level and go up, up, up. Your mouth opens into a narrow O, and when you look at me your bottom lip is curled, worried.

"I been school now. Go home?" you ask, hopefully.

My heart aches. "No, Sweetheart, you're going to stay all morning, like we talked about." I have a smile on my face—*see, Sweetheart, this is going to be fun!*—but I'm on the verge of tears.

I hope you can't see them. "You're going to make new friends, and play games, and learn lots of new things."

You take a moment to process, a frown appearing on your cute little face. "But, Mummy, I know everything. I can read!"

Aw, Sweetheart … You know your alphabet from A to K, but after that you get confused and try to fit T in at least three times. Still, it's a hundred times more than we ever hoped.

"It'll be fun," I insist, as your hand squeezes mine even tighter.

At home, I have a box of tissues, a slab of chocolate and a film to watch, to distract me until it's time to pick you up.

There are other children and parents gathering now. Mums, dads, grandparents; every one of them has the same proud/petrified/frenzied expression on their face, the same fervent tone in their voice. Every one of them has the same flatness in their eyes as me.

The gates open and two young, smiley teachers appear. Just kids themselves really—oh, I feel so old.

"Hello! Come in, come in. Mums and dads, you are welcome to come as far as the doors, but the children will go into school by themselves. If you prefer, you can say goodbye now."

Your hand stays firmly in mine. Your little body shakes, vibrating against my legs. I sense that saying goodbye here is not an option. I guide you forward, you shuffle your feet.

"Hello Cassie," says one of the teachers, walking towards us and kneeling down to you. "Do you remember me from when you visited last term?"

You nod, glancing at me for confirmation. There's a knot in my stomach. It's time. In a moment, you'll let go of my hand and disappear inside. I take a breath, and hope I can keep the tears at bay a couple minutes longer.

"Can you hold my hand and show me where your peg is?" says the teacher. "You drew that beautiful fairy, didn't you?"

You nod again, a little more certain now. Slowly, you peel your fingers from mine and hold onto your new teacher's. You instantly look more grown-up, more like a little girl than my baby.

I never thought you'd get this far. After your abrupt entrance into the world, the doctors warned us you'd need constant care, that you might never learn to talk, let alone manage to go to school. You astounded us all. You can walk, talk, draw. You dance and sing and play intricate role-playing games with your teddies and dolls.

And here you are, dressed in an oversized uniform, carrying a book bag that's almost as big as you. You look up at me. I bend down for a hug.

I'm not ready to let you go.

New Clothes

The shop screams at me, painted in lurid graffiti, with bold colours and 3D effect lettering, seizing my attention. Overbearing music makes me want to walk straight past. I don't. I'm curious. I've passed this shop so many times. Today, I linger, staring at the window display, gathering the courage to enter.

I'm an unwavering M&S shopper, an innocuous Next girl. But sometimes I get bored with being safe—I want to be wild and different. Shopping in a place with such a *distinctive* style *is* wild and different, right?

The lights are dim when I enter, and my eyes take a moment to adjust. My ears, to be honest, will take longer.

You stare at me with cool indifference. I try to ignore you, browsing the elegantly-sparse racks instead, running my hands across clothes that are far too expensive. I hide behind a tall shelf unit displaying sky-high stilettos, hoping you'll just forget that I'm here.

"Can I help you?" you call in a brusque tone, trying to intimidate me. You're wearing the same cerise dress as the mannequin in the window—you're just as slim, just as plastic.

"No thanks." I want to outstare you, but I'm too timid, too bashful. Just so you know, if I was more confident, I'd stare right back at you.

I shuffle backwards and sideways, camouflaging myself behind lime green jumpsuits. I become deeply engrossed in a red dress, focusing on that instead of you. It's beautiful. Knee-length, strappy, low-cut with beading along the neckline. The fabric shimmies and dances—it feels like fresh air. I can imagine it cascading across my hips. On the hanger, it's half-realized, a mere indication of its true potential. It needs a body inside it, to make it perfect.

You're bored, glaring at people walking past the door. Few of them peek inside, and even fewer enter. This isn't the type of shop that gets packed out, I presume? For the most part, it's just you and me. You'll be out of business by the end of the year. *What a shame.*

The fabric of this dress is so delicate, I can't help but let my fingers brush over it again. It folds up surprisingly small and slips into my bag without any effort at all.

I don't leave straight away, that's always suspicious. I browse the jumpers laid out on a table, and the overpriced jeans. I pick up a skinny pair and hold them out in front of me.

You're suddenly beside me, sneering. "I don't think we have these in your size, *do you*?" Your eyes scan my generous curves, and you extract the jeans from my fist.

"Well," I say with a smile, "bye, then." You stare after me, eyes dull and harsh. You pout.

I won't wear the dress. You're right, *none* of the clothes in your shop are big enough for me. But I'll take it home and hang it in my wardrobe with all the others.

In the Beer Garden...

… you sit and chat, effortlessly.

… you sip cider or beer or wine.

… you settle back in the patio chair and let the sun warm your skin, shielding your eyes. You push your sleeves above your elbows and roll up your jeans, exposing tanned ankles.

… the bees nestle among the roses and birds sing, competing with the rising laughter of children as they dangle from the climbing frame, as they play hide-and-seek around the Wendy house.

… the 14th century pub looms over you, an imposing stone building that boasts several reported ghosts. Occasionally, you glance up at one of the windows, as though a movement has caught your eye. You watch.

… laziness presides.

… I sit alone.

… my hands shake, my eyes are puffy and raw. I probably shouldn't be here, in full view of other people, but I didn't know where else to go.

… you don't approach. You glance away embarrassed, pretending you haven't seen me. I notice you, though. I see your uneasiness, your concern. You think I'm a violent drunk who will make a scene, who will hurl abuse at everyone, forcing you to shepherd your children away from me.

… actually, I haven't had a sip of my drink yet. It's sitting on the table in front of me, the glass dripping with condensation. I'm afraid if I try to pick it up, my hands will shake so much I'll pour lager over myself. Also, I'm waiting for someone. He hasn't arrived yet, but when he does I want him to know I don't turn to drink *every* time.

... I know I'm being foolish. I know it's been one attack too many. I know I shouldn't be waiting at all. I could go inside right now and phone my dad. I could tell him I want to come home. He'd be here in a flash, jumping over cars and houses to come to my rescue, the way *you'd* be there for *your* kids. I'm someone's kid, you know.

... my bruises are starting to emerge. The sun makes them conspicuous, deep blue and brown against my pale skin.

... I really wish you'd come and ask me if I'm okay.

... I don't move. I don't go in search of a phone. I don't search for bus money. I don't do any of the things I dream about doing. He'll come and get me soon, smile at you as he squeezes his hand around my arm. A warning that I shouldn't run out on him like this.

... I take my first sip of the lager, soothing and familiar. More than likely, I'll just get up and go home by myself. You won't even notice when I slip away. You'll watch your kids, be engrossed in your conversation, buy another round.

... you'll completely forget about me.

The Love of a Good Woman

"Are you a good woman?" you ask as you sit down.

I hesitate. The others have introduced themselves, even though their names are printed on the badges stuck to their jackets or t-shirts. Some have tried to use a cheesy chat-up line, sealing their fate—they're too ensnared in their own brilliance, and I deserve better than hackneyed phrases. They've taken their seats awkwardly, or overconfidently, or with a sneer as they realize I'm not blonde, busty and twenty-one.

I've made snap judgements on them, too, of course, and you're no different. You haven't looked at me—you place your drink on the table and fuss with the card in your hand. You fidget with the chair, pulling it close to the table, then push yourself away again, making everything *just right*. I'm not sure any woman will be good enough for you.

My hesitation turns into a pause, which transforms into a long, awkward lull.

"It's a simple question"—you peer at my name tag—"Evie. How can I plan a life with someone who can't even answer the basics?"

You're a joy, aren't you? No wonder you're single. I take a sip of my complementary wine. It's far too sweet; I keep forgetting that.

"Is—is that what you're looking for then, a long-term relationship?" I ask.

"Aren't we all?"

I lean towards you across the table and lower my voice, inviting you into my confidence. I read a dating book once—it said this was a fool proof technique. "I don't think most of these men are, judging from the conversations I've had."

I glance to my right, at the twenty-something guy who just left. He'd outright propositioned me. He's now repeating the same question to the shy, hapless woman at the next table. I wonder if he knows I can hear every word. If we all said yes, his bed would be crowded later.

You don't respond. You follow my glance with disinterest.

"How old are you?"

The question drags me back to this table, *this* conversation. "Thirty-six." I'm no longer embarrassed by this. I used to get coy and blush, find a way to avoid answering. But I've settled into my skin now. I'm happy. I certainly don't feel thirty-six.

"Kids?"

"No."

"Would you like them?"

A trick question. "Would you?"

You smile tightly, irritated. You make a mark on your card. I try to read upside down, but you notice and hide it with your other hand.

I take advantage of your distraction and ask, "What do you do?"

"I'm an accountant."

"Oh." You don't look like an accountant—you have a semi-sexy smoulder, though it could be disdain. I wish I had a witty comeback for *accountant*. "That's, um …"

"I should stop telling people my job, shouldn't I? I always get the same reaction."

"It might help. Until you're engaged, at least. Perhaps spy would be better, or Batman?"

You smile again, more genuine this time, more relaxed. I think I might be breaking you down. Soon, I might get to talk to the real Arthur.

"Is that your real name?" I ask. I'm sure some people use aliases—Precious, the girl I walked in with, for example. And

Captain Jack … that can't be his real name. Harkness or Sparrow, though? I'll have to ask him when it's our turn together.

You stiffen. "Of course it is."

"Sorry, it's just … a bit old-fashioned." *Evie and Arthur; Arthur and Evie …* I imagine writing our names on joint Christmas cards.

"My grandfather's name."

"Sorry," I say again, and we pause. I glance at my watch. Another three minutes to go. "Have you done this before?"

"No."

"Why now?"

"It's time. My wife …" You stop and stare at the table. You consult your card and make another note. You close your eyes for a moment. I wish I knew what was going on in your head. "What would be your perfect date?"

"A picnic. On a summer's day, by a river. Lazy and relaxing. What about your wife?"

You redden, scratching at the corner of the card. "She died."

"Oh, I'm sorry," I apologize *again*. I want to leave, right now. One stupid comment after another. I'm bad at dating. I should stay single, should buy a cat … several cats.

You shake off my sympathy. "It was a long time ago. Not important."

"Not *important?*"

"I meant, my feelings about it aren't important, not that she wasn't …" You disappear into a memory—your eyes glaze over, a melancholic smile plays on your lips.

"I didn't mean to pry." I rest my hand on yours. You don't pull away.

"I didn't plan—I haven't so far—mentioned my wife at all," you mumble, still avoiding my eyes, and I wish you wouldn't. After a moment, you take a deep breath and glance down at the card.

I sit back, pulling my hand away from yours. Maybe I left it there too long. Did I? You didn't extract yours either.

I sneak glances towards the other tables. No one else is holding hands. Some couples are laughing, but mostly they are suffering through stilted silences and monosyllabic dialogue. Like us.

"Do you like opera?" You revert to your stock questions—a disappointment.

"No."

"Ballet?"

"No."

"Justin Bieber?"

I laugh. "No! Do you?"

"God, no. I was just making sure. You can't be too careful these days. Women in their thirties are weird."

"I hope I'm not."

"Well, you passed the music questions with flying colours, so you've made a good start." You wink, I blush. "What *do* you like, music-wise?"

"Rock, metal, grunge, and, um …" I sigh. "Glam."

"That 70s shit?"

"Yeah. Am I weird now?"

"You're teetering on the edge."

I giggle. I like you. You're careful, not giving anything away, keeping a check on your emotions. But you're truthful, you really *are* looking for something permanent—it's not a line. Of all the men I've met tonight, I'd choose you—if I had to.

"I don't think I've laughed properly all evening. I've been doing a lot of that polite, fake chuckling."

"Yeah, women have been doing that to *me* all night too." You frown melodramatically, feign taking offence.

"I can't believe that."

You shrug. "I know. Bizarre."

I take another sip of my too-sweet wine. "Yuck, I don't know why I'm still drinking this stuff."

"It can't be as bad as this lager. May I?" You indicate my glass and I nod. You wince as the wine hits your tongue. "Oh, no, that is so much worse." You hand my glass back. "So, have *you* done this before?"

"Once or twice. It never came to anything. I guess I never expected it to."

"But you came back tonight?"

"Yeah." I don't explain. You've been reticent, now it's my turn. "Maybe it's just not my fate, to meet someone, to settle down. Do you believe in fate?"

You shake your head and I feel foolish. Next I'll divulge my overreliance on horoscopes and how I wouldn't be here now if today's hadn't been favourable. You're silent. The seconds tick down.

"My wife … she said I should find a good woman. Sadly, we had a long time to discuss it." You look at me. You don't smile. The bell rings. You're supposed to move on, but you don't seem to have heard it. "Are you a good woman, Evie?"

"I hope so."

When It Rains

I usually love watching the rain. I'll sit on the large chair beside my bedroom window as it drives into the glass. Sometimes I'll lie down and stare up at the sky, closing my eyes to listen to the melodic pattering of the rain so it seems to fall down upon me.

I'll wrap myself up in a soft, fleecy blanket and read a good book. I'll drink coffee during the day and wine in the evenings. On snowy days, I'll drink hot chocolate with lots of little marshmallows.

Tonight, I'm not reading, or drinking. I'm not curled up comfortably, staring at the rivulets running down the window, at the streaks of orange as they catch the streetlights. I'm waiting for you—and you're late.

The weatherman said we were due four days' worth of rain in the next twenty-four hours. It feels like we're getting more than that. The weatherman didn't mention the gale-force wind. It's pulling slates off roofs and unpitching tents across the south coast. The local bridge is closed to high-sided vehicles.

I can hear the metallic clattering of someone's dustbin knocking against their wall, and the whistling sound of the wind down the chimney. It's alarming, disturbing.

"Don't travel tomorrow," I told you last night, over the phone. "Wait a day or two, until the weather's better."

"I'll be fine, it's just a bit of rain. I've been away too long already. I'll see you at four."

"I love you," you said, almost as an afterthought. Not quite an *afterthought*, but we've been together for so many years, we tend not to say it so much anymore—we just know.

I glance outside, pulling back my net curtains. It's not *just* raining now—it's bouncing off the road, thundering down with the strength of a monsoon. As I watch, it turns to hail, tiny balls of ice laying thickly on the road, making it slippery and risky. People, walking past on their way home from work, run for shelter as ice bites against their skin. Two teenage girls squeal.

I wish you were here. You're *driving* in this, and if you haven't hit the hail yet, you soon will. The skies will darken and your visibility will reduce. I imagine other people, not as careful as you, losing control of their cars and sliding into you. I see you ending up on the wrong side of the motorway, crushed against the verge and a Subaru.

The hail has reverted to rain, still heavy. It looks like it's in for the night.

I check my mobile, hoping you've stopped at a service station, and texting me from the warm café, drinking coffee, treating yourself to a chocolate brownie. I glance at the phone every couple of minutes, desperate to hear that beeping announcement.

I sit on the edge of the chair, gnawing at my thumb nail. The street is empty now—no one wants to be out there in this. Apart from the people who have no choice.

Apart from you.

The H Word

They say I shouldn't say I hate you. Specifically, I shouldn't say it to your face, although saying it behind your back is equally as bad, apparently. So many rules!

They say it will hurt you, that it will drive you to do something bad.

My therapist says I should be nice, because being nasty is a bad thing. Treating me like a child. I *AM NOT* a child. I'm nineteen, an adult. I'm allowed to drink and vote and get married, and do whatever the hell I like. I know how I feel—and I know I hate *you*.

I avoid you as much as possible, scarcely looking at you if I catch a glimpse. Pretending you don't exist.

But sometimes, when I can't help it, I'm drawn to stare at your fat thighs, your ugly face, your huge tits swinging in front of you, entering rooms before you do. And your stomach! It sticks out so much you look pregnant *all of the time*. You're a disgrace.

When I wake up in the morning, when my guard is down and my head is still foggy with sleep, that's when I'm most likely to see you. I'll catch sight of you in the reflection of my telly, grey and distorted. The way I always see you.

(I don't have mirrors in my bedroom anymore, although Mum refuses to take them down elsewhere in the house. When she's out, I cover them with towels.)

So you're there, mirror-imaged in front of me. You put your hands on your waist and stare out of the screen defiantly, like you don't care. Your fingers don't even touch when you do that. I've seen girls on the internet whose fingers actually overlap. Ha! See, *that's* how fat you are.

I want to tell you over and over: *I hate you, I hate you, I hate you.*

I don't care if it hurts you. It *has* to hurt, because that's how you'll gain the courage to go even further. I don't care if you hide beneath your comfort blanket, or gorge on your secret stash of chocolate. I don't care if …

Wait, what are you doing?

This is new.

You're holding a kitchen knife, the blade against your wrist.

Put that down, you don't know what you're doing with it! One wrong cut and you'll bleed out all over the carpet. You'll lie on the floor as the life drains from you, from me.

From us.

I hold my breath and wait for you to make that decision—the decision that will affect us both.

Ode to River

You were on my wall, held up with sticky tape. One of the (many) posters contained *fun facts* like your star sign, your favourite colour, your hobbies. I stuck my favourite picture up level with my pillow, so I could see you as soon as I woke in the morning.

I loved you so much. Or, as much as anyone can love a picture of an actor taped to their wall.

I loved your smile, and the way your beautiful blue eyes followed me around the room. I talked to you, sharing my problems and dreams, my fears and teenage angst. I stared at you as I fell asleep and then dreamt about you. I remember always waking up just a little disappointed.

But, you know what? I never saw a single one of your films. I was underage, and looked far too young to get in to the cinema with fake ID. Later on … I guess I lost interest.

I never heard your voice, never saw you walk or break into laughter. You were on my wall, frozen, serene and pensive—just a gorgeous guy, watching over me as I slept, and did my homework, and argued with my best friend, and raged at my parents behind their backs.

Always there, always smiling—with your hair falling across your face—concentrating on your guitar or notepad. I always wondered what you were writing.

I was going to grow up, move to Hollywood, and marry you … of course.

But then, you died.

I read about it in the paper, with my parents tutting over my shoulder because drugs were involved. I got lectured about the dangers, as though I might run out and do drugs just because you had. As though I couldn't see your death as a warning.

Later in my bedroom, I fell to the floor and sobbed while you watched. My tears, uncontrolled and abundant, stung my reddening face. Finally, when I'd depleted my energy, I lay there and looked up at you. I reached out and touched your cheek— you nestled into it.

I was going to marry you but you left me—the whole world— behind. And it was such a senseless thing to do. Eventually I took down your posters.

I grew up and replaced you with that guy with a saxophone.

This Is My Love Story

Me and you, at the end of the world.

And oh, how beautiful it is. We sit high on the side of a mountain, our legs dangling over the ledge and watch comets hurtling toward us. Up here, we gaze across hundreds of miles of broken landscape, and trace the curvature of the horizon. We look down through a blanket of clouds and pretend we are angels.

As the comets strike, craters form and dust billows. Volcanoes spurt molten lava, spraying it into the air. Tsunamis smash against the shore, and colossal surges of water push inland. Life is obliterated. The sky burns red and orange and purple, the Earth blisters.

Except …

… it's not like that at all. The end of my world will be more sedate. My bones will ache, I'll grasp for oxygen. I'll lie beside you and share my final secrets. It'll be slow—there will be no explosions of any kind. I'll close my eyes and fall into an endless sleep.

"How do you think the world will end?" I ask, leaning back and staring at flighty clouds tumbling past the window.

You open a packet of jelly babies and offer me one. "Zombies. I think they'd be fun."

"Fun?" I scoff, biting off the head of a yellow one. "All that running?"

"Okay, then, how do you think it'll happen?"

"Fire and brimstone. Something dramatic and beautiful."

You shake your head. "Too scary."

"And zombies aren't?"

"At least we'd have a fighting chance."

"I wouldn't know what to do."

"Because you don't watch enough telly—they all know how to fight on TV."

You flip idly through the pages of *Woman's Own*. I stare at the ceiling. I'm hungry. I hate waiting. I hate waiting rooms.

"I've seen the future," I say, then groan a little, because really you're the last person to say these things to.

"Are we going to win the lottery?"

"No, not our future, everyone's future. I saw the end of the world. As real as anything."

"A dream. They've been getting more vivid, you know that."

"No, I mean …"

But you've already turned away—intent on an article about women who commit murder during menopause. Your jaw is tight, eyes glazed. Normally, you'd be reading out quotes and making comments, so I know you're not reading—I know you're just ignoring me. I reach out and hold your hand. I'm sorry.

You smile after a moment, then glance up at me and wink.

The appointment with the consultant occurs in slow motion. You do most of the talking—asking about treatment plans and next steps—until your words become garbled. I forget to listen after a while. I disappear out of the window and stare at the trees, at a squirrel fluttering along the branches.

He scrabbles around, grabbing leaves and climbing to the highest, flimsiest of branches. He bounces there for a while, then gets startled and vanishes.

You're still talking, you and the doctor. You're both looking at me; I nod, as though I'm listening.

The comets are coming. I can see them falling through the atmosphere, burning up like tiny stars.

"Come on," you say afterwards, as I stand without purpose in the corridor outside. "Let's go somewhere. We can talk."

I follow. In truth, I'm not really here. I'm out there, with the comets, with the craters and dust storms. You take my hand and suddenly we're sitting in the car. I close my eyes, just to stop the world from turning.

When I open them, you've driven me up to the moors. We're parked beside the road, and ahead of us is our usual tor—whenever we go for a walk on the moor, we end up here. From the road, it seems huge, sliding into the blue sky, cutting through the clouds. It's not that big really, just a bump in the horizon. Even so, when you reach the summit, you can see out as far as the coast or across into Cornwall.

Up there, you hear nothing at all. Up there, we could be the only people left.

"Ready?" you ask, and I nod, because this is the only place where I'm safe from the comets, the tsunamis, from the cancer skulking around my body.

We walk past the ponies, oblivious to us in their search for tasty grass. We pause to catch our breath as the hill gets steeper and rockier. We switch from walking to striding to hiking over the course of a few minutes. The higher we climb, the more I forget. The rocks turn into boulders, into large granite mementoes from the past.

Or maybe they're comets that have already landed while everyone looked the other way.

I sit on one of the highest, flattest rocks, and you produce a picnic from your bag. You've packed all my favourites: tuna and coleslaw sandwiches, mini pasties, bacon quiche. I want to devour them all—because I would have, before—but I feel nauseous. I take a sandwich and linger over the crust.

"Something else? There's more—I made plenty."

"Maybe in a minute."

You eat a sandwich in three bites, and delve back into the bag. "I brought cider."

"Lovely." I don't care if I feel sick, I need to taste that. You took me to a cider festival for our first date; we giggled over the curious names of local ciders, like Janet's Jungle Juice and Orchard Pig Philosopher, and danced all night.

You crack open two bottles of Fanny's Bramble—our subsequent favourite—and pass me one. I anticipate the taste—so much better than the tuna sandwich that I'm still mangling. Food is insipid now, random textures that glue my mouth together.

But the cider ... Oh, boy, does it taste good. Sweet and sharp in equal measure, with subtle bubbles that make my sinuses tingle. You laugh at me, and tap my nose the way you've always done. I drink and stare out to the sea, amazed—as always—that I can see a whole city in front of me, that I can hide the whole city behind my hand.

You watch me moving my hand around. You know what I'm doing, we've discussed it at length before. I love that I don't have to explain myself—I love that you've been in my life.

It shouldn't have been this way. I got sick and wasn't supposed to. We were going to go travelling—our bags packed, tickets bought, adventure ahead. Until suddenly, it wasn't. We shouldn't be here, we should be in New Zealand by now. Should be at the top of a mountain, looking down on the clouds.

Me and you, at the bottom of the world.

"I've made a list," I say, lying back on the granite slab, using the bag as a pillow. Fuzzy clouds scramble across the searing blue sky, criss-crossing the higher cirrus clouds. They tumble, transform—they resemble dogs and Australia. They dissolve as the wind steals them. "Look ... that one looks like the Tardis."

"A list of what?"

"Of women. To date when I'm ..." I can't say it. "Or marry. You probably want to get married someday, don't you?"

"I want to marry you."

"Sorry, you're not my type." I tickle your ribs so that you know I'm joking. I close my eyes to prevent the tears that are fighting through. You've never mentioned marrying me before—you've never asked. This seems an inappropriate time to bring it up. I don't want to have one of those deathbed weddings either. I don't want you to start our life together as a widower.

"So, this list …?"

"A colleague at work, an old friend from school, that girl at Starbucks—"

"The one with all the tats?"

"No, the cute blonde."

You watch me, but don't reply. Perhaps you don't like blondes. I've never asked. You sip your cider and look out across the moor. Below us, the reservoir is deep blue. Beyond that, dark green forests nestle into valleys, and other tors rise up, grey and stark, on the other side. It's a rough terrain, unchanged for centuries, if you look in the right direction.

We're completely alone. We could witness the destruction of the world, and escape it. We could lose ourselves up here, run away, never look back.

"I'll miss this." It just slips out, I didn't mean it to. I have moments of trepidation, where the future seems more important than the present. But I will. I'll miss your touch, your laugh, your brooding silence when you're angry. "What will you do? Afterward?"

You tut, camouflaging your exasperation. We haven't had a proper fight for a long time. I miss that too.

"There is no afterwards."

"Of course there is, for you, for everyone. You'll carry on." I take your hand and entwine our fingers. "I have to know. I want to picture you doing something amazing. I need to know you'll be all right."

Your face softens. "You shouldn't be worrying about me."

"So, tell me what you'll do when I'm gone."

Your smile fades. You stare at the reservoir below us, then lift your head and gaze out to the horizon. "I'll raise money for charity, a bike ride maybe, or a marathon … I'll stop eating junk food, in your honour … I'll learn to water-ski, because I've always wanted to try that …" You pause, take a breath. "And I'll visit your parents on your birthday, every year, until they dread me coming because it"—your voice splinters—"it reminds them of the daughter they lost."

A tear slides down your cheek. I've never seen you cry. You brush it away, but another follows. And another. Eventually you stop wiping them away. My own tears are on the brink, but we can't both break down. This only works if one of us is brave at a time.

You puff out your cheeks and allow the air to escape slowly. "I didn't realize I'd thought about any of that." You reach for another couple of ciders from your bag, open them, and pass me one. "Here. Drink."

Time passes. The wind grows stronger and the temperature drops. We stay until the sun begins to set, until the sky burns red and orange and purple.

Me and you, at the end of the world.

My House

This is *my* house!

You have *no right* to be here!

You removed my furniture, took my dresser that had been passed through generations of women in my family, and threw it onto the dump. You moved your own rickety, flat-pack junk in—temporary and cheap, hideous in my beautiful house. It'll collapse in a few months, bits dropping off here and there. Mine would have lasted into the next century at least.

You cleaned, painted, scrubbed. You opened windows and set bowls of potpourri about the place to freshen it up. Then you hoovered, scrubbed again, opened doors to allow the air to flow through.

But it's still there, isn't it? The lingering smell? A mixture of lavender and mothballs, of old age and rotting. You've checked the attic for dead mice.

It's me. Whenever you smell that musty lavender, it's me, stalking you. I'm gliding through your walls, following you from room to room, invisible. When you feel that prickle on your skin and quickly turn around? That's me, too.

Did the estate agent tell you I died in this house? In the master bedroom, to be precise: I fell asleep and never woke up. You feel it, I know you do, the ominous chill when you're in there, the one that leaves you unnerved and restless.

I bet they didn't. Estate agents are ruthless like that, aren't they? Anything for a sale. You asked all the questions you were supposed to, about the damp proof course and dodgy wiring and local schools. But you didn't get around to the one question people *ought* to ask, and somehow never do: *how many people have died in this house?*

And now you're stuck with me. Or I'm stuck with you, more like.

No one opened the window, you see. No one was there at the moment I passed to let my spirit leave. No one was there for several days, or maybe even weeks. Once you die, time has little meaning, of course.

I stirred when I heard the front door being battered down. There'd already been knocking, and the sound of letters delivered. The phone rang several times a day, too —mostly cold-callers, I expect. Not friends, not people who'd noticed I was absent and wanted to check that I was okay.

Those small disturbances, I could ignore—they didn't last long. But that thudding, echoing around the house, and the voices shouting outside my window, roused me.

The firemen and police covered their noses when they came into the room. I didn't look my best. They paused for a moment, staring at me as though I was the first body they'd ever seen. I'm the first body I'd ever seen. I was shaken. My skin was parched, my lips drawn back from my teeth. My eyes were sunken and blackened. But I looked peaceful—I'd had a quiet death.

Carefully, respectfully, the firemen placed my corpse onto a stretcher and carried it downstairs. They slid me into the waiting ambulance, while the neighbours watched. But they forgot to take me. They shut up the house, nailing boards across the windows and doors, and I couldn't get out.

Sisters

The bride is stunning, radiant and beautiful beneath her veil. She glides down the aisle, a fairy tale ending to her whirlwind courtship. Look at her, unable to contain her joy. Look at how her groom gazes at her with such love and awe. It'll be such a blissful marriage, filled with laughter and babies and love. Sometimes you just *know*, don't you?

Oh, this must be *killing* you. It's usually you, isn't it, at the centre of all our attention? It's *you* who people normally stare at and admire, falling over themselves to talk to you. The rest of us gave up years ago. On nights out, in pubs or clubs, men will literally push past us to get to you. When you're around, the rest of us might as well not even exist.

Apart from Tom. You saw him first, you were all over him that night, but he wasn't keen. It was embarrassing, watching you try to get him to notice you. He preferred your sister, couldn't take his eyes off her. You tried everything to lure him away. But your flirting became more and more blatant, more and more pathetic. Nothing worked.

No one laughed; no one smirked—honest!

When you went up to the bar again, they quickly left, slinking away via dark corners. I saw them go. In fact, I *encouraged* them. It was good to see her happy, even better to see the look on your face when you realized what had happened.

It's got to be tough for you. Is it? *Is it* tough to watch her walking down the aisle toward her true love, her happy-ever-after?

You're wringing the Order of Service card in your carefully manicured fingers; your face twisted into some kind of bizarre smile. You're reduced to the pews because the bride was convinced as a bridesmaid you'd overshadow her.

She's probably right. And you were banking on being in the wedding party, weren't you? You could work that angle, the up-for-anything attendant, copping off with the best man or an usher. Maybe you could even belatedly catch the eye of the groom himself, and make him question his whole marriage.

But she's got her best friend's two little daughters instead. They walk carefully behind the bride, making sure they don't stand on the train, and remembering to smile like they've been told. They're dressed in flouncy chiffon, just like the Disney princesses they love so much. Their eyes are fixed straight ahead, mildly apprehensive of all those cameras focused on them.

You won't be in many of the photos, just a couple of the official ones, and even in those, the bride will make sure you're nowhere near her.

The procession has reached the altar. Look at her, *really* look. She's glowing, she's poised and graceful, the epitome of a blushing bride.

She's always been second best to you, always skulking back into the shadows. She really shouldn't be up there, should she? It should be *you*. You're the beauty, the party-girl, the top of everyone's guest list—the woman who makes every night out extraordinary.

But, the bride is one thing you are not.

She is happy.

Picture of You

You cradle a mug of hot minestrone soup, and squeeze a chunk of warmed bread between your fingers. Butter drips onto the plate and down your chin when you take the first bite. You jump at each rumble of thunder, curling your legs even further into yourself, biting on your lip and glancing out of the window.

Your hair is wet, framing your face with thick tendrils. I took your sodden clothes when you came in, and gave you my robe. It's too big for you—it reaches half-way down your shins and the sleeves fall over your hands, as though you're shrinking. You're wearing my woollen socks too, because you complained your feet were so cold. Your smooth white legs peek over the top. You look like a teddy bear in need of a hug.

You haven't noticed that I'm sketching you. You're staring down into the mug, smiling. You run your hand through your hair and encounter a mass of knots. I watch for a moment, amazed at how this perfect woman could be with such an imperfect man as me. Because you are—perfect, I mean.

Another flash of lightning swamps the room. Thunder follows closely behind.

You shudder. "It's so near," you say uneasily, laughing to disguise your anxiety.

"Not that close. We're safe in here."

My pencil falls across the page, forming a black and white likeness that you'll refuse to look at. *Nooo*, you'll squeal when you realize what I'm doing. *My hair's too messy, I'm not wearing makeup. Stop it!*

You'll hide your face with the sleeve of my dressing gown, and push back your hair. I'm trying to show you that you're beautiful, even without makeup, *especially* without makeup. Always, every day, perfect.

You won't believe me, though. You'll say I'm lying, say I've drawn someone else. It's not a photograph, you'll say. *Photos* don't lie—men with pencils and paper lie.

I draw your eyes last, almost impossible to duplicate. And in just grey-scale, I really can't do them justice. Blue like the ocean, like the midsummer sky, like a sapphire hanging from a chain around your neck. But I can't catch your sparkle, your soul, no matter how hard I try.

Soon, I'll reach over to you and kiss you softly. Soon, I'll tell you that I love you more and more each day, and that I want to be with you forever. I'll ask you to move in with me, so that I'm there every time there's a storm.

But not yet.

First, I'm going to finish your picture.

Insomnia

I stare at the cracks in the ceiling, at the shadows looming down.

You're snoring beside me, strident yet unsteady.

Dawn arrives, stretching across the sky, creating a paint box of reds and purples, until the sun pushes over the horizon.

Another day, I tell myself, deflated. Another night passed, notable only for its lack of sleep.

I drag myself out of bed and into the shower, make a pot of coffee and bring you a cup. All the while, you're sleeping.

I nudge you as I walk around the bed. "Wake up."

You groan and turn over. "It's half-six," you mumble.

"I couldn't sleep. I'm going in early." I glance at the mirror, and jump back with mock horror. "Once I've raided my make-up bag, of course."

It's dull outside, after that flamboyant sunrise. Storm clouds gather overhead, although the rain's holding off for now. The sun remains hidden all day—the dense grey light making my office darker than usual. At lunchtime, during my walk around the nearby park, my limbs grow heavy. I travel home in gloom.

You cook—my Friday night treat. I can barely taste it. It feels like glue in my mouth. I try to hide my aversion, but apparently not enough. You finish your meal in silence, and swipe my half-eaten plate from in front of me.

I watch TV without any idea of what's happening. I'm so tired, but I can't sleep. You're out. I should've gone with you, but when I said I didn't feel like it, you stormed out and told me to suit myself. You don't get that I don't choose to feel this way, that I'd do anything for just a couple of hours' sleep.

"Thanks for caring," I yelled at the closed door. I stood there for a while, wondering if you'd come back. You didn't.

Eventually, before nine, I get into bed with a glass of wine and a book. Tonight, I enjoy neither. I go through the motions of happiness, convincing myself I am.

With the wine gone and the book discarded, I lie still and close my eyes. I don't have to sleep, right? I can just lie here in peace, and relax. My head fills with past embarrassments, ripostes I wish I'd made in ancient arguments, childhood fears, regrets, unrequited loves. I create endless lists of groceries, of things to throw away, of holiday ideas.

Stop!

And I do. My head falls silent, and the room is stagnant. I am a void, a vacuum.

I remain restless.

It's colder tonight. I snuggle beneath the duvet and tuck my knees up into my chest. I still shiver. I get socks and a jumper from my drawer, grab my bobble hat from the chair. I feel like an arctic explorer.

When you come home—two, three o'clock in the morning—I pretend to be asleep. You bang cupboard doors, clatter crockery, in search of a snack. You *sshh* yourself loudly, and giggle. You find every single creaky step and floorboard as you tiptoe upstairs and into our room.

You're asleep as soon as you lie down, snoring, growling at me from your dreams.

Dawn spreads across the sky again, fingers of light touching the night and pushing it away. Not as intense as yesterday, but enough, just enough.

I slide out of bed without looking at the clock. Today is Saturday. No work for either of us, and therefore the time has no meaning. I leave you to sleep.

My limbs are stiff, leaden. They ache, becoming immobile. I make coffee in slow motion, every movement requiring individual consideration. I feel unwieldy, as though my puppeteer has grown bored of me and left me in a knotty heap.

The toaster takes forever to pop, and when it does the toast is black. I scrape the charred crust off the bread, then dump the whole slice in the sink and stare at it. The tap drips.

My hands refuse to grip—I want to drink my coffee, but I can't pick up the cup. So I leave that too.

And upstairs, I hear you, tossing and turning, and snoring. Always snoring. Mocking me with your ability to sleep deeply and unaffectedly. Louder and louder, drilling into my head. Just for a second, I imagine the silence of smothering you with your own pillow.

Of course, I won't. My hands aren't working today, remember?

Early risers start to amble past the house, to the corner shop or to the park with their dogs. They're all wearing grey this morning. A strange choice for a dull day. They peer in through the window, scrutinizing me. They slow down, they loiter. They want me to know they're there, always watching.

"Hey, you're up," you say sleepily, leaning against the door frame.

You have a tousled sexiness in the mornings, your hair ruffled, your pyjama bottoms hanging low on your hips. There's no sign of last night's aggravation. You stretch, showing off your torso. Not so long ago, I would have kissed you and lured you back to bed.

"I've been up for a while."

"You should see the doc."

"I'm fine."

You look at me for a while, considering me closely. You're waiting for me to crack and tell you all the things that are wrong.

Except, nothing's wrong. Apart from not sleeping, apart from my hands not working and the world becoming nothing but several shades of grey, everything's just as good as ever.

Although the people spying on me are still around—they're a concern.

But I won't tell you about them, either. You'd stand at the window and say, "Where? I can't see anyone." And they'd all hear you and know I was on to them. I'd have to drag you away, which is far too much effort.

So I sit still, curled up under a large fleece throw and try to warm up. You bring me a hot water bottle and turn on the heating. You make hot chocolate and sprinkle dark chocolate flakes on top. And then you sit beside me and help me drink, because my fingers are fused in one position.

"I'm worried about you."

"I've just had a couple of restless nights, that's all"

"It's been over a month."

"Don't be silly. Last night and the night before."

You shake your head. "No, love."

It's Saturday. It's Sunday. It's Monday. It's the end of the week and the start of a new one. I watch the days pass, but don't participate. I stand at the window and don't remember how to leave the house.

You cook and clean. You get frustrated with me and yell. I stare blankly because your words don't make any sense—they are a dull throbbing in my head.

You're grey. The light is grey. Life is grey. I want to hide beneath my large fleece throw. I swaddle myself within it.

I close my eyes when you're not here, but I cannot sleep. I listen to cars speeding past, to hordes of kids going to and from school. I hear the silence.

I don't even move upstairs to bed anymore. What's the point when the days and nights simply merge into one entity?

Tonight, long after you've gone to bed, there's a light outside the house. It shines too brightly, too vividly to be a streetlight. It pierces through the grey, and creates something beautiful, a prism of colour like nothing I can remember.

I'm drawn to the window for a closer look. There's no obvious source. Around it, the night is a thick swathe of fog. I step out-side, onto the garden path, and walk toward it. It moves further away, down the road. It leads me, one footstep at a time.

Soon I am several hundred yards away from home, several miles. Jacketless and bare-footed, I keep following, completely absorbed. On and on, I walk until I forget the pain.

The Person Walking Toward Me

The beach is deserted, save for a couple of dog walkers down by the rocks. They throw sticks into the sea, and the dogs dive in, splashing around with excited barks. The sky is grey— the sea, and my mood, matches it. I almost stayed in bed, but I'm only five days into my New Year's resolution. It's far too early to give up.

I kick up the sand with each step, focusing on my wellies— bright red with pink flowers—making gouges into the beach.

Back up on the coast road, a dark figure leans against the old rusty railings and gazes out to sea, looking out toward the lighthouse.

Is it you?

I haven't seen you for so long, it might not be. It might just be a random person stopped to look out at the stormy water. Even so, I quicken my pace slightly. I stop looking down at the sand and keep my gaze fixed on you.

Have you noticed me? Are you waiting up there for me? Are you checking to see if it's me, *really* me, before you quicken your pace toward me? Will you sweep me up into your arms and swing me around?

I don't recall how long it's been. From this distance, you haven't changed at all. I have. I've got wrinkled skin, a weary expression and grey hair—I wear it in a bun now! Can you imagine? Of course, you won't have to imagine soon, we'll be face to face.

I wonder what I'll say.

I wonder how you'll explain yourself.

You start walking in my direction. I want to run to you, but the combination of soft sand, wellingtons, and a dodgy hip would cause calamity. I keep my steady pace.

Should I shout your name? I listen carefully, in case you're calling mine. I don't want our voices to cancel each other out. And anyway, the wind is whipping around me, and carrying all sound out to sea. I can't hear the dogs barking anymore, even though they're still paddling in the same spot.

Do you remember what you said the day you left? You said you'd marry me as soon as you found a job and a flat. You said you'd write to tell me how it was going, and when you had some money, you'd come back and ask my dad for permission.

You said you wouldn't be able to sleep at night without saying goodnight and giving me a kiss under the lamp post outside my house.

I waited for you. I'm wait*ing* for you.

When did this beach get so long? I've been walking for ages, and we're not getting any closer to each other.

Suddenly you're right there in front of me, nodding fleetingly in greeting, walking past without a second glance. It's not you. I catch my breath—my heart stops for a moment. My legs wobble beneath me. I resist turning to watch you—*not* you—walking away from me.

I knew … of course.

I knew it wasn't you.

I remember watching the news that day, the day you left, the day I waved you off at the station. A body had been found in a toilet cubicle at Waterloo Station, beaten up, mugged. The police appealed for witnesses, but they were vague with the details, ambiguous. I turned the television off and pretended I hadn't heard anything.

You never sent for me. You never called or wrote. I knew you wouldn't.

Beware Strangers

I am your shadow. You can't see me; I'm behind you, waiting for you to turn and catch me out of the corner of your eye.

I've always been here, watching you grow, maturing from the kid who always had scraped knees and played football in the street with the boys, to the graduate who feels out of her depth in her first job. I've shared every birthday, heard every whispered wish as you blew out the candles. I saw you fall in love with your first boyfriend, and—I admit— cheered when you finished with him because he was such a jerk.

I've witnessed *all* your stupid mistakes, wanting to stop you but not knowing how.

You're making another one—another mistake—right now, accepting a drink from a stranger. He's slimy, shiny, far too smooth and self-assured. He eased onto the stool beside you, and made some lame joke about pork scratchings. You laughed! *Stop laughing, you fool!* Turn away; go back to your friends.

He passes you the cider you asked for when he offered. "Cheers."

"Cheers," you say, lowering your eyes demurely.

"Do you come here often?"

I groan; *you* laugh … again. "Do you use that line often?" *And does it work?*

He laughs, holding his hands up in acknowledgment. "I just meant I'm here all the time, and I haven't seen you before … Okay, okay, that was bad. I was flustered. I don't do this often, chat up beautiful women in bars." He pauses, evocatively, waiting for you to register the compliment, and gazes into your eyes. "But when I saw you, I just knew I had to meet you. That's …" he pauses again, "okay, isn't it?"

Creep! Get out of here! But you're not listening to me, of course. Why would you?

"Uh-huh," you say, catching your breath, trying to control your excitable heartbeat. "I wouldn't know a good chat-up from a bad one, to be honest."

"A gorgeous woman like you? I don't believe it."

You blush clumsily. You really *are* out of practice, aren't you? It's embarrassing. But I suppose that's why you're falling into this tragic conversation.

He clasps your wrist and strokes his finger along your arm. It's probably that tingly feeling that's making you simper, making you smile and accept another drink.

Here I am, sitting behind you as always, powerless to intervene.

When he invites you to get something to eat with him, you say yes. You wobble off the stool and collapse into giggles, into his arms. He holds you tight.

"Oops," you say. "I think I've had a little too much to drink."

"Yes, I think you have." He smiles with indulgence. "Come on, let's get that meal."

I can't stop you, of course—I'm just your shadow.

Floating Away

During my first session, you told me to lie back on the couch, close my eyes, and imagine myself floating in a boat. You gave no limitations.

It was such a simple request, and yet I struggled. I could picture a lake, a rowing boat, a mountain range soaring up into the sky. I could see a figure inside the boat, but it wasn't me. I wasn't in the boat. I was looking down on it, an omniscient viewpoint.

I tried to dive into the boat, tried to make myself heavy, so that I'd sink down and land softly inside it. I tried to walk down the mountain and swim across the lake to reach it.

It took three hour-long sessions before I managed. I was finally inside the boat, lying on the bottom, those wooden sides enveloping me. It felt so right; I *belonged* in that boat, staring up at the narrow strip of blue sky that was visible. I was so excited, I almost knocked myself back out of the visualization.

You told me I'd made huge progress, that you were proud of me. I was gratified.

The idea behind these sessions was to help me overcome my depression. But I cheated. My replies to your questions were what you wanted to hear, not what I was really feeling. When you asked me how I was each time, I'd say *fine, good*. When you asked me whether I still had those debilitating suicidal thoughts, I said *no*.

But you must have known. After all your years as a therapist, you must realize people lie to you, because the truth is too devastating to admit.

At night, I began to dream I was on that boat. I fell asleep bobbing on an ebbing sea. Each time I closed my eyes, I saw myself on the boat, until I began to feel more comfortable *there* than *here*.

"Well," you said, cheerfully, on the day I was discharged, "take care. Keep up the good work."

You handed me a card with my out-patient appointment on it. My face fell. "It's with a different doctor. Not you?"

"I only work with in-patients. It's time for you to move on. It's a *good* thing."

It felt anything but *good*. I nodded like I understood. But I didn't. You didn't want me anymore. I needed you, but you were abandoning me, and I was going to be alone.

A week later, on the day of my first out-patient appointment, I went to the river instead. I sat on a bench and stared out at all the boats floating on the water, bobbing gently as the tide pushed them around. I recalled the peace and tranquillity of our sessions, your melodic voice guiding my dreams. I remembered how serene I'd felt in your care, in my boat, and—sitting on that bench—I was home.

I don't know when I stood up. I don't know why I decided to walk down to the water and wade out to the nearest dinghy. My jeans, dragging through the water, weighed me down, but I was determined.

I climbed in, and untied it from the buoy. There were no oars, so I used my hands to push myself out past the row of other boats, moored up and waiting. As long as I was clear of the boats, I didn't need oars—I never had them in my dream. I could just allow myself to float out on the tide.

The wind was stronger downstream. I lay down and stared up at the grey mottled sky, at the low clouds scurrying along. The boat danced on the water.

Further and further away from the shore, out past the headland, past anywhere that could still be called the river. Out to sea. I was tossed about, flung against the sides. I clung on so I wouldn't tip out. Finally, the wind died down, the clouds parted, and the sun came out.

The boat bobbed smoothly. Satisfied at last.
I'm still out there, to this day.
Probably.

Growing Apart

The café is almost full—it's half-price for pensioners on Tuesdays. I wish I'd known before we ducked in to get out of the rain. I grab a tiny table over by the window, while you queue for our soup and bread roll. The relentless thudding rain outside means thick homemade bacon and lentil soup is the perfect lunch.

I watch the elderly couple nearest me. They sit in silence, knife and fork carefully placed, a small jug of water untouched between them. Neither of them speak. They gaze in different directions.

They've run out of words, I realize. Probably married for so long, they've said everything they could possibly want to, or need to say. How sad.

You're still in the queue, tapping your fingers on the counter. You smile at me and roll your eyes. You make subtle hand gestures to indicate your irritation at the dithering lady in front of you. I can't help giggling, you always make me laugh. We've been together for five years. I don't ever want to stop laughing with you.

The waitress brings out two plates of roast chicken to the silent couple. They both look up at her and smile, murmuring their thanks. They make a small remark about how nice it looks, then return to their subdued indifference. At least now they have a distraction.

How long have they been married? I estimate forty years, forty-five, perhaps? They fell in love, raised children, overcame money worries together and holidayed in the same hotel each year. *He* worked hard all week, out of the house for twelve hours a day—commuting and working—and played golf early on Saturday mornings. *She* had a strict timetable of chores, attended coffee mornings, and volunteered at the charity shop one day a week. She shopped for groceries every three days, pottered in the garden and gossiped with neighbours, and read Barbara Cartlands while the dinner cooked.

Then he retired.

They were forced together. Their plans for foreign travel and regular trips to London were cut short with his unexpected heart attack, and now they only have weekly lunches in their local café, choosing the same meal each time. They have a bubbling resentment that neither of them will admit.

You're at the head of the queue now, paying, flirting with the fifty-something waitress. You're tall and athletic and your brown hair is getting unruly. You are funny and charming, and when you look at me and wink, even across a roomful of OAPs, I blush. I *never* want to sit opposite you and have nothing to say.

You set the tray on the table and start moving our cups and teapots onto the table. I reach up and kiss your cheek.

"What was that for?"

"I love you." And I start talking, ten to the dozen, about every subject I can think of.

On Waking

I wake with a start—as though I'm late, as though thunder has ripped through the sky, as though the cat has landed squarely on my chest.

It's 1:35 a.m.

None of those things have happened.

I breathe heavily and a hot sweat creeps across my body. I listen. Something is wrong, but I don't know what. Strange shadows dance on my wall. The streetlights outside are dimmer than usual.

I remember now. You were trapped, buried alive in a collapsing building, and I couldn't reach you. Couldn't save you.

You called out for me, frantic and fighting. I clawed at the rubble, but it kept replenishing, sucking you away. I screamed your name until my throat rasped. You yelled back at first, becoming fainter, more distant, until I couldn't hear you anymore.

In reality, you're beside me, snoring softly, your hand contracting a little as you dream, your expression relaxed. I guess your dreams are happier than mine. I want to wake you and tell you that I'm sorry I couldn't rescue you, but that wouldn't make any sense. I want to tell you I had a nightmare, and have your sleep-sticky arms wrap around me, reminding me that you're safe.

But I don't. I lie facing toward you, watching your eyelids twitch. I reach out to touch you, just in case.

Angel

"Oh, it's you." I pause for a moment and consider the implications.

You don't say anything. I don't expect you to.

"Please, come in." I smile. I don't suppose people smile at you much.

You step into my room and look around. You're not as assertive as I expected.

"You've come for me, haven't you?" I cough, wheeze, catch my breath—my breath really isn't worth catching anymore. Oxygen doesn't have the same impact as it used to. "Well, you took your time."

You sit on the edge of my bed. It's oddly reassuring. I wasn't sure what to expect, but this feels right. I want to reach out to you, but you'd probably become mist beneath my fingers.

The pain in my chest is getting worse. I try to move, but it causes a shooting pain around my body. I hold my breath, but that only makes it worse, spreading out towards my arms and legs, like ice in my veins. I hate feeling like this. I hate my body crumbling away.

"Help me."

You rest your hand on my chest. Warmth radiates and the pain evaporates. I relax, easing myself onto my pillow. I listen to the rattle in my breathing.

"Thank you."

Normally, I'd press the alarm beside my bed and several nurses would come running to my aid. They'd pump me with more drugs, plump my pillows, and ensure I was seated at the right angle to see the television. They'd make me comfortable and bring me a cup of tea.

It's beyond that now, though, isn't it? Beyond tea and comfort. That's why you're here.

You pass me the glass of water from my cabinet. You support my head while I sip, and lie me back down gently. The pain is returning, a dull ache, a burden. My eyes feel heavy.

There's a different sound to the ward at night. Everyone whispers; the sound of footsteps echoes and lingers in the corridors. The darkness has a sound of its very own, like a lullaby.

"I'm not sure how this works," I say after a while, because you are still mute, and I don't know if you're waiting for me to do something profound. You're making me nervous all over again. "Does it hurt? At the end … will I feel it?" It's a shallow question. I wish I hadn't said anything. "I'm scared."

You look at me with such overwhelming love. Your eyes soften and you rest your hand on my arm. Suddenly I hear all your words, spoken at once. I am enveloped in serenity and peace. Nothing matters anymore. Everything is forgotten. My body is ageless, uncluttered by the past.

You nod, just once, and we rise up together. I look back at the body on the bed, a good body, *my* body. I am aware of the monotone sound of the monitor, and the nurses running into the room. I wish I could tell them that I'm okay, that I'll be okay for always.

They work on my body, trying to bring me back with urgency. But I don't want to go back, I want to go forward. You pull slightly, and we walk together toward my eternity.

Decisions

I sit in my car at the junction, and can't decide which way to go. Every morning I sit at this junction, and every morning I make the wrong choice: I go to work.

Every day, I sit at my desk on the second floor, and go through the motions. I'm not even sure I make a difference anymore. I just plod along until home-time, like a kid waiting for the school bell. I spend all my time dreaming about the weekend, yet, when those transient two days arrive, I'm too tired/too busy with housework drudgery/too caught up dutifully visiting my parents to enjoy them.

How did I get here? How did I become so middle-aged and responsible?

Do you remember when we spent afternoons in bed and evenings in the pub? When every day was a brand new holiday? When we stayed awake until dawn, talking about our plans for the future? When we realized we were kindred spirits and I asked you to marry me as the sun rose on that chilly October morning?

Something changed, right then, in that moment. Getting married meant being sensible. It meant getting a mortgage and using our savings to put down a deposit. It was *the right thing to do*, said your dad. Getting a steady office job was *infinitely more reliable than painting*, said mine. You don't know this, but they both sat me down and said that I needed to grow up and become a man.

They took our ambition and joy, screwed it into a ball and threw it across the room. They wrapped us up in forty-hour work weeks and pension schemes and five percent interest rates. They made us consider houses near the good schools, even though *neither of us wanted bloody children*.

Every morning, I take a moment longer than required to pull out onto that junction. Just that little bit longer than the day before. People have started beeping at me, or abruptly pulling out around me and gesturing their irritation.

I still make the wrong choice: I still go to work.

But one day, soon I hope, I'll make the right choice. I'll phone you, on your way to *your* boring office job, and we'll both head back home to spend the day in bed, and the evening in the pub. I'll drag out my paints, and you'll pick up your guitar, and we'll try really hard to remember who we used to be.

Fast Asleep

You hold my hand like you've always done. I can't feel it, but I *know*. I hear you say my name.

I don't answer. My eyes are closed, and they'll remain that way. I'm locked into this half-dream that I don't understand. But you're here, and whenever I hear your voice, my dream is happier.

"Oh God," you sigh, anguished and hopeless. "Please wake up, please, please … I need you."

You've been saying the same thing for weeks, but it's not helping. There's nothing you can do. It's out of your hands.

You stand and walk to the window. I know this, because you say, "It's sunny today. I got so wet on the way home last night. It's getting colder, too. And the leaves are almost all gone. There's a mist this morning, one of those low, lingering ones that you love."

Autumn, then.

I've missed summer altogether. No holidays, no walks on the beach or barbeques, or late night dancing at music festivals, no extended evenings, drinking too much sangria.

Time is fluid in my head. I've been asleep equally forever and for only a few minutes. I don't remember how I got here.

"So, I guess it's time for the news, the Telegraph today, for a change. Is that alright for you? Ready?" Your voice is upbeat and jolly, but tense, tired. I think you must be here a lot. "The Scotland referendum is next week. It's all over the front page, and the second, and third, and … well, you get the idea. Kate Middleton's pregnant again. Erm …" You rustle the pages. "England beat Switzerland. You're not interested in that, are you? I am. It was brilliant … Okay, sorry, no more football."

You don't say anything for a while. I'm used to it. Sometimes it's because you've left for the night, or gone to get a coffee. You drink a lot of coffee when you're here, I can smell it. Sometimes it's because you're staring—at me or out of the window—and you've run out of things to say.

I wish you weren't here so much. I feel bad. Surely you must have better things to do, a girlfriend to see, friends to meet up with. You're holding my hand again. You're leaning over me and kissing my cheek. "I'm going now, time for the bus. Goodnight, my love."

You're my best friend, and I've always known you wanted to be more. When I wake up, we should go on a date.

How to Be a Facebook Friend

Your status reads: **I don't believe it. So cross right now :-/**
    Someone comments almost immediately: **What's up huni? :-) xx**
    You say: **I don't want to talk about it.**
    I hold my mug of hot chocolate in both hands and settle back.
    The next comment: **Aw huni. Im here for u <3**

There are a few likes, and a whole stream of identical comments follow, dripping onto my news feed gradually over the next ten minutes. You've disappeared, though.
    I leave my laptop open while I flick through satellite channels. Saturdays are ridiculously bad for telly, unless you want to see some blokes watching football and talking about it. Or if you're into black-and-white films, like your granny used to make you watch, full of women with impeccable skin and sharply-pitched voices. Or if you can handle ten hours of the same program, any program.
    My choice is Doctor Who, original series nineteen, starting with Castrovalva: Part One.
    My eyes dart back to check my news feed updates.
    Someone seems to be posting *all* of the photos they took on their holiday to Greece, and someone else is taking every quiz possible. They're sharing the results too: they have a green aura, and should have been born an Aries in the 1960s. They have a really rubbish knowledge of classic books, but know a lot about music in the 80s. I'm not sure I need to know this.
    And … you're back: **Some people need to learn some manners!**
    Again, no explanation, just a random isolated statement, floating down my feed.

A whole heap of people you don't know jump in to offer supportive messages and little heart shapes. They don't *care*, you know, they're just being nosy. They don't care about you because they barely know you.

I have a feeling that doesn't matter to you, though; the comments count is growing, which means people know you're popular. Job done.

You: **My life is so hard right now.**

But at the same time you're posting photos of a recent night out, of far too many pouting selfies, solo or with several pouting friends. Yeah, your life looks really horrendous. How *do* you cope?

I don't expect you've noticed, but I'm not commenting. I'm not playing your games. We were friends at school, and at some point last year you went on a mammoth friending spree, gathering up as many names as you recognized.

We haven't spoken since—since school *or* since you friended me. We don't mutually *like* each other's statuses, we don't tag the other in old class photos, or share funny cartoons on each other's timelines.

On the telly, Peter Davison is running about a bit. I think I've missed some important part of the storyline.

You're having a clash now, with someone who dared to suggest you were just attention-seeking, and my mouse hovers over the *like* button.

My hot chocolate has gone cold. Perhaps I ought to share that with the world? I wonder how many frowny faces and {{hugs}} I'd get for that revelation.

Instead, I just unfriend you, and make another drink.

Leaving (Again)

In another minute or so, you'll be just a distant figure on the platform. It's nice of you to see me off, unexpected. Our eyes meet and we smile awkwardly. You glance at your watch. You want to leave now, and honestly, I don't mind if you do—*nice* has turned into *painful*.

But you remain there instead, rocking on your heels, and tucking your hands into your pockets.

A garbled announcement explains the delay. It's an excruciating end to an agonizing couple of days.

"Mum died," you said, ten days ago, your call cutting into the stillness of my flat.

"I'm sorry to hear that."

"I was wondering … I don't suppose—"

No. Don't say it. Please don't ask.

"—you would …" You'd paused and sighed, unable to articulate the request. I wasn't sure if it was grief or the memory of our parting that thwarted you. "She was always fond of you."

"Don't you think it would be weird? We haven't been together for over three years."

You were silent on the end of the line. I wandered into the kitchen, and switched on the kettle. I'd found a clean mug and a teabag before you replied.

"She doesn't have anyone else."

No, she wouldn't have. She was isolated, hidden away, never the same after your father died far too young. She barely left the house. She lost contact with her family years ago, and seemed content with being completely alone. She was vaguely hostile with anyone who tried to befriend her, suspicious of them, fearful. It surprised me, after everything you'd told me about her, that she allowed me into the house, let alone become a friend.

As it was, we were the only people there, at the funeral—just you and me. And I realized that you probably don't have anyone else either. I can easily picture you sitting in her chair, in her house, and never leaving.

Last night, as we drank the wine, we toasted her life.

"So ..." I said, and faltered in claustrophobic silence.

I'd planned to go straight home after the funeral, but when I saw your strained, distraught face, I knew I couldn't leave you alone. We found a tin of tomato soup, and some bread that needed finishing up, eating the remains of a dead woman's pantry.

"It was a nice service," I said, trying to make *some* conversation.

"No, it wasn't. She deserved more."

"Why did you call me?" I wasn't going to ask. I *shouldn't* have asked.

You looked bashful. "Honestly? I don't know. It was all so sudden, and you were the first person I thought of. I needed to hear your voice." You stared into your glass. "Look, I ..."

I held my breath, waiting for the words that would have me staying here with you, falling back into our life together.

Three years ago, when I left, I had exciting plans. I thought you were holding me back, making me miserable. But I'm still stuck. I have a few friends, but no new partner, not even a cat to keep me company. I waited for those words ... you begging me not to leave again. But they never came.

We sipped the remainder of our drinks and said goodnight.

And now I'm waiting for the train to pull away. The holdup is making this perplexing situation worse. You're avoiding my gaze, making this far too hard. *Please leave. Please just leave me alone.*

You look at your watch again, running your hand through your hair. You look conflicted. Your eyes meet mine, at last, and you smile a little, taking a hesitant step forward. I touch the glass, touching your face.

The train starts to move, at last. You get smaller, but I imagine you running after me. It's what I want. The train rounds the bend, and you disappear from view.

Redemption

I see you over there by the jukebox. I wave: you pretend not to see me. Our parts play out meticulously, and we'll go our separate ways.

In a couple of months, we'll bump into each other again—your turn to wave, mine to look away.

We were friends once—at school—can you believe it? How many years ago?

"Too many," you said, on one of those rare occasions we were compelled to talk to each other.

"I know, right? We must go for a drink. I'll give you my number." And I did. You never rang. I never expected you to.

Today, right now, you leave your spot by the jukebox and push through several people at the bar. You're heading straight toward me. *Shit!* Is it too late to run away, to head for the exit, to involve myself in deep conversation with the guy standing behind me?

"Debbie!" You air-kiss my cheeks. "How great to see you! It's been so long."

"It has."

You brush hair away from your face, and I catch the sparkle of a large diamond on your ring finger.

"Engaged?" I squeal because I'm expected to. "Congratulations!"

"Oh, thank you. I'm so happy." You stare at the ring as though it's still a surprise. Your gaze rests on my left hand. "What about you?"

I nod. "Yes, I'm happy too."

"Engaged?" Your face falls for a second. You pout. "Married?"

"No," I say. "Happy."

We stand in awkward silence. We have nothing further to say to each other.

"Listen, we really *must* meet for lunch, soon." You pull your mobile from your bag, and hand it to me. "Put your number in here."

I consider giving you a fake number, but I don't. I can't think of any numbers other than my own.

"I'll phone you, I promise." You play with the buttons, attaching my name to my number, I assume, then glance over your shoulder. "I must go." You pause, mid-turn, and squeeze my arm. "It's good to see you."

I watch you walk back to your friends, and I turn back to mine.

"Who was that?" they ask.

"Someone from school. She's either dying, or thinks I'm someone else."

They laugh, but actually I can think of no other reason for what just happened.

―――――――――

I don't expect you to phone, but you do.

"Are you free on Saturday? I know a lovely place."

"Um, sure …"

"Great. I'll text you the address. I'll see you at one."

I stare at my phone long after you've disconnected, wondering what the trick is. Will you be sitting in the café opposite, pissing yourself laughing, while I wait for you in the rain? Will you take bets on how long I'll stand there? Or perhaps you'll order the most expensive dish and run out on the bill?

You did that once, remember? It was one of those times you were pretending to be my best friend. You said you had birthday money and wouldn't it be fun to go to a grown-up coffee shop for lunch rather than Burger King? You said you wanted to treat me, because I was such a good friend, but you disappeared before the bill came. I had to phone my mum—in tears—because I didn't have enough money. I was grounded. I missed prom because of you. Remember?

But we're older now. You're engaged. You might even have turned into a nicer person. I should give you the benefit of the doubt, *shouldn't I?*

Saturday arrives before I'm ready. I stand in front of my mirror, in my best dress, and look hideous. I'm probably wearing something you wear to clean the bathroom—or something you clean the bathroom *with*.

Perhaps make-up will help.

Uh. No.

I pull on the boots that leak and hope it won't rain. This will have to do. I look as good as I can.

I'm ready far too early. I pace around the flat, listen to the radio, dance to Blur, jump up and down, and swear loudly into the empty room.

At twelve, I catch the bus. I stand in front of your "lovely place" far too soon, and wait.

And wait.

People bustle past.

Umbrellas go up around me.

I slink further under the awning, trying to protect my feet. A chill wind sweeps in along with the rain. I zip up my coat.

And I wait, becoming more dispirited as the minute hand of my watch ticks to quarter-past. Perhaps I was right after all, and this *is* just a stupid joke.

"Oh, Debbie," you call out, hurrying up the street. People move to give you an easy path. "Have you been waiting long?"

You air-kiss and smile brightly. I stand still, my arms folded. You offer no explanation or apology.

"Shall we go in?"

You wait for me to open the door, then walk through first. You allow the waiter to seat you and pass you the menu. I take the opposite chair, gazing around at the sleek black-and-white décor, the leather-backed chairs, the demur lighting, the prices …

"I've never been here before." I glance down at my dress and feel like a bag-lady.

"Really? How surprising."

I ignore your tone. "So, I'm curious why you wanted to meet up so desperately."

"Not *desperately*. I thought it would be nice."

"But we've never … done this before."

You shake your head and laugh. "Of course we have!" You glance over the menu. "Wine. We should have wine." You point mid-way down the wine list. "A bottle of that." To me, as I scan the menu, you say, "You *have* to try the chicken—it's divine."

I smile at the waiter and order the cannelloni. You sneer slightly.

"Vegetarian?"

"No."

In silence, we watch other diners. I await your conversation, but none is forthcoming, and the tension is grating. I play with my fork, until I catch your disapproving glance and feel like a three-year-old.

"Do you see many others from school?" I ask eventually.

"A couple. Melody and Jennifer."

I shudder: the trio reunited. The school bullies colluding over Chardonnay and chargrilled chicken.

"How nice."

The wine is served. I'd like to down the glass in one go, but I control the urge. I swirl the wine around.

"What do you do?" you say. "You work, I presume?"

"Yes. In a bookshop."

"How quaint."

"People will always read books."

"I don't understand people who have time to read. They mustn't have any friends at all."

I temper my reaction with a curt smile. I reach for my wine glass and drink some more, and then a little bit more. At this rate, I'll be sloshed by the time my cannelloni arrives. I put the glass down carefully, aligning it with the angular pattern on the placemat.

"What about you?"

"I'm a personal shopper. It's how I met my fiancé, actually." You glance at your finger again, and sigh with contentment. "He wants me to give up work as soon as possible, of course—"

"—to start a family."

"Oh, good God, no." Apparently the suggestion is completely ludicrous.

I smile weakly. "Personal shopping? That sounds glamorous."

"Oh it is. Just look at all these things I get to borrow."

"You're allowed to borrow stuff?"

You tap the side of your nose, and wink.

"I love your jacket," I say. I don't mean to, it just comes out.

"You have to have the right figure to carry it off, of course." Your tone is caustic, disguised in a smile. "Do you work out?"

"No."

"I love my yoga classes. I wouldn't be without them."

"Mmm …"

Our meal arrives. Your chicken, my cannelloni. We eat demurely, picking at the edges as we make small-talk. I still haven't figured out why I'm here, but the more I drink, the less I care. The bottle is empty. You order another.

"For lunch?"

You smile. "Why not? We're celebrating."

"Celebrating what?"

"Us ... Finding each other again."

I revert to my original conviction: you're either dying or you think I'm someone else.

"I love your earrings too." They're huge, gaudy, gold, and probably more expensive than they look. I hate them—I just needed to change the subject.

You pause, then take them off. "Have them, take them. Go on," you insist when I protest. "They're mine to give—I didn't borrow these."

You hold them in the palm of your hand, thrusting them toward me. I take them from you and inspect them carefully. "If you're sure, thank you." I lay them down on the table between us. "How's your chicken?"

"Delicious."

"You haven't eaten much."

"I'm savouring." You cut a small piece and chew. "Better?"

"Yes." My own plate is almost empty. "Your jacket ... I'd love to get one of those."

"Oh, Debbie, I doubt you could ..." *afford it*, hangs between us. You look uncomfortable, blushing intensely beneath your make-up, I imagine. I stare at you with a smile, belying my understanding.

"You should try it on," you say.

I lay my knife and fork on the plate, finished.

"Go on, this colour would really suit you." You take it off and stand up, encouraging me to do the same.

I slip the jacket on.

"It fits," you say with surprise—feigned or otherwise. You pull my dress tight across my torso, and scrunch the excess up in one hand. "We're about the same size. Look at your waist —it's tiny. You shouldn't hide it beneath such ... shapeless clothes."

"You said I was fat at school."

Your face falls. "Oh God, you remember that?"

"You don't forget your bullies."

"I thought—hoped—I'd imagined it." You slump down in your chair. "I really was a bitch, wasn't I?"

I nod. What else can I do? I won't lie to save your feelings. I watch you crumble, while I pour more wine into our glasses and drink. I don't give you the relief of breaking my gaze.

"I'm so sorry, Debbie." You squirm. "I often think about you, about how I treated you. I brought you here to make up for it."

"It won't. Nothing you do will make up for how you made me feel all those years."

You have no words. Finally.

I take another drink and smile. "I like your skirt."

"Oh, you should try it on. It goes perfectly with that jacket."

I laugh. "I can't try *that* on at the table."

"Let's go to the Ladies, before dessert."

I try not the show my astonishment at the grandeur of the toilets. The room is bigger than my living room; it has two chaise longues and an abundance of hand creams in the corner. On the walls are several large abstract prints, and mirrors with gilt edging.

We are alone in here. When you talk, you echo slightly.

"I want to make it up to you properly," you call through the cubicle door. With a bit of rustling, the skirt is held up for me to collect.

"Uh-huh." I slip my dress over my head, and drop it onto the floor. I avoid looking at my pale, bulging thighs in the mirror. I pull the skirt on. It nestles on my hips and swishes against my knees. I button up the jacket. Immediately, I look slimmer. You wore a camisole beneath it, but I show cleavage. I scoop my hair off my neck and fashion it into a loose bun.

"I want to blah blah," you say.

"Yeah, hmm." I turn in front of the mirrors, catching my reflection at different angles. My eyes are drawn to my hips, to the perfect shape the skirt has created.

"Blah blah blah …"

"Sounds good," I murmur. I look too good to waste in front of a mirror.

You have to know, I didn't plan this. But once the thought appears, I can't help myself. I know I should take off your clothes and return them—you're still talking, using words like *friends* and *happy* and *apology* over and over. The cubicle door between us allows you the freedom to confess all of your sins.

And it grates—your voice, your self-pity. I feel nothing for you.

I grab your bag and take several twenties from your purse—not all of them, I want you to be able to settle the bill. I delete my number from your phone, fold my discarded clothes into a neat pile, and leave the restaurant the way you once left me.

Missing

The helicopter's circling again. A few of the neighbours stand in their gardens, mugs of tea in their hands, staring up at it, looking concerned and congregating in small groups. No further news, though. They're just recycling what we all already know.

It started at first light. Yesterday, my Twitter feed mentioned a missing child in our small town. It has to be connected. I turn away from the window with a stomach-turning sensation. It's hovering now, out over the fields on the edge of town.

"Oi, come on, breakfast!"

You thud down the stairs. "I was watching the helicopter," you say. "They're looking for Bradley, aren't they?"

"Do you know him?"

"Not really. He's in my year, but …"

I freeze. It could be you. On another day, it could have been you who went out with your mates and didn't come home. It could have been you who they're searching for now. My boy, my baby boy. Bradley: someone else's baby boy.

I re-boil the kettle and pour the water into two mugs, watching the tea swirling around. I add milk and throw the teabags into the sink.

We sit with our breakfasts in front of us, but neither of us is eating. The fluttering sound passes above. We both look up to the ceiling, picturing its path. Finally, the sound dissipates. The kitchen is silent.

"It's so awful. His poor mother. She must be in pieces," I say softly.

You shrug. You're a fourteen-year-old kid, after all. I don't really expect anything more from you. You've probably got your thoughts all lined up, but you just can't express them. I remember being your age—you want to say the right things, but the pressure is immense, so you shut down and stay in the corner.

"You won't … You wouldn't …" *You wouldn't disappear, would you, if—say—we had an argument and I grounded you? You wouldn't run away and leave me wondering if you were still alive? You wouldn't do that to me, would you?*

"Mum," you sigh, long and exasperated.

"Sorry. I know. It's just … I worry about you. It's my job."

You reach across the table and hug me. "Love you."

It's back, the helicopter. The noise permeates the house again, going over the same areas, proclaiming the search is all but pointless. They should have found him by now, with all their heat-seeking equipment, shouldn't they?

Later, when you've gone to school, I walk the dog. We take a different route from our usual one, glancing down dark alleys and checking beneath overgrown hedges, doing my part. I don't know what I'll do if I find something. I hope I don't.

True Love, 2015

I love you. There, I've said it! Is it too soon? I don't *think* it's too soon. I'm just so happy. Okay, we're miles apart, and—technically—we haven't actually met yet. But you're coming soon, and I know you feel the same.

We fell in love during our first email chat. You don't have Skype yet—you're such a techie dork, you didn't even know what I was talking about when I mentioned it—but that's okay, I don't *need* to see you. I fell in love with your personality.

Anyway, I've printed out the photo you sent me and pinned it up on my wall, so I can see you when we message each other. I've put it into a frame next to my bed, too, so I can look at you last thing at night and first thing in the morning.

My niece says you look a bit like that actor, Jason Statham, but I can't really see it. You have a much sexier smile.

You've done the same thing with my photo, you said so. Of course, you can't pin it up anywhere, because you're undercover at the moment—on track to crack an international drug cartel, and when you do, you'll be straight on that plane to me (a matter of days, you said). But you've printed it out and put it in your wallet instead, so I'm with you wherever you go.

I never thought someone like you could ever be interested in someone like me. I've been alone for such a long time. I work long hours, seeing the same people every day, I don't go out with friends—I barely have any, and the ones I do are married with children.

When we first connected on that dating forum, I was attracted straight away. Usually I'm so careful—sceptical and cynical—but you were different. You were funny, a bit mysterious and cautious, yourself. You'd been hurt before, and wanted to make sure you only fell in love with someone special. You didn't talk about yourself much, but you asked about me, you were *interested* in me—it made a change.

You'll be arriving soon. I've bought new bedding for us, for our first night together. I've sent you the money you asked for, for the flights. I was a bit suspicious when you mentioned that, I can tell you. Colleagues at work told me you were a fraud, but you aren't, are you? It's just that being undercover for so long means it'll take a while to get your paperwork straight, and you can't wait that long to meet me. You said so.

I'm looking forward to feeling your arms around me as you sweep me off my feet at the airport, to showing you off to my family, to starting our life together. I'm looking forward to replacing your photo on my bedside cabinet with a picture of *us*.

Circle of Chaos

I have no idea what's happening.

Come with me, it'll be fun, you said. *I've been going to this group for a couple of weeks, and I think you'll fit in perfectly.*

So now I'm here, following you down the dark steps into a basement pub. I head for the bar and order a large glass of wine. I start drinking before the barman hands back my change. I hate meeting new people.

"Ready?" you ask, and I follow tentatively.

You're immediately enveloped into the small group over in the corner, and I'm left on the side lines. I pretend like I'm happy alone, that I'm caught up in my own thoughts.

"Hi, I'm Ananke." A woman with bright red hair reaches for my hand. "You look lost—you're new, aren't you?"

"Er, yes." I scan the room for you. You're talking to two other women. A third is standing alone, intent on her mobile. Every so often, she glances up and watches, without attempting to join in. She has an angular severity to her—she's a little scary, to be honest.

"That's Aphrodite, she founded the group."

"That's … that's an unusual name."

"We don't go by our real names, here. Nicknames are given to us when we join. Did Nyx not explain?"

"Nyx?"

"Your friend." Ananke nods in your direction.

"Right. No, she didn't. She didn't tell me very much, actually." I don't want to be here, I don't like it. I want to go home. "Um, why do you need nicknames?"

"So we can't be traced." And she winks before guiding me across to sit in the small booth beside you.

Before I came out tonight, I made dinner for Husband and Son, unloaded the dishwasher, and made sandwiches for tomorrow.

Before that I helped with Son's homework while I ironed. Before that I was at work, waiting for the day to end.

"Tell us about yourself," Aphrodite says, and the circle closes around me.

A moment ago, everyone introduced themselves. *Demeter, Hera, Nyx, Ananke.* I smiled and nodded at each in turn. I sipped my wine, unable to shake my apprehension.

Five pairs of eyes on me. I hold my breath.

"How would you describe yourself?" Aphrodite prompts, reminding me that a question had been asked. And everyone urges me on.

"We've all done it," you say with a smile. "We've all shared our stories."

Stories? I don't have stories. I look around the circle. "I'm married. I've got two kids, one away at university, the other in Year 11. I'm a school secretary." I shrug. "That's it."

"But that doesn't describe *you*." Aphrodite leans forward and rests her elbows on the table. "Do you know how I describe myself? I'm enthusiastic, occasionally extrovert, shy with strangers. I have phases of mania, I suppose you'd call it, where I have so much energy I can't fully expend it—I end up jumping up and down on the spot, squealing excitedly. I fall in love too easily, and get hurt too much."

I lower my head, embarrassed by her disclosure. I can sense time passing, eyes focused on me. After a while, after my silence has become painful, Ananke flicks her bright red hair and says, "So … I completed my task, this week. It's Wildfire Red. I might go green next time."

The group collectively admire the eye-catching hair, as though they hadn't all noticed it when she first walked in. They forget about me, and I am relieved.

Aphrodite moves on to Demeter. "How was your week?" she says, nudging Demeter's arm. "Did you do it?"

Demeter looks sheepish. "Yes," she says in barely a whisper. She turns to me. "I told the group last week how I always wanted to have sex in the afternoon. My husband is a lights off, after-the-news kind of man. On Saturday, I ... well, I jumped him!"

"Yeah? Awesome!" Hera makes a whooping sound—a full-on hands-waving celebration. She sinks down when she realizes no one else has joined in.

Some of the other drinkers glance across, then return to their own lives.

My eyes widen. I can't hide my shock. I am definitely *not* suited for this group.

Everyone else toasts Demeter, with a more subdued cheer. She basks in her new-found daring.

I realize how little I know you, if this is what you ... if you think this is what *I* ... Oh no, oh no. I grip the table. I'm just about ready to run away now.

You notice my horror and laugh. "We're not all ... I mean, that's not what the group is about. We all have different reasons for being here." You sigh and turn to Aphrodite. "It's your baby, you explain it better."

"Do you ever think back to the person you used to be, the girl you were before you grew up?" Aphrodite asks.

I consider. It's been a long time.

"Well, we give you permission to do all those things you've forgotten you wanted to do."

"I don't need permission." I pull back slightly. You smile and nod encouragingly—you're completely sold on this. I wonder what *you've* done, and then shudder, because I don't think I *want* to know.

"So, you're completely happy with your life?"

You snort. "Yeah, sure she is."

I nudge you, affronted. You have no idea whether I'm happy or not. "Yes. I am, actually."

Aphrodite holds up her hands. "If you are—if you *truly* are—I salute you. You're the first person I've met who doesn't want something more." She looks at me inquisitively, forcing a smile. She looks perplexed.

The conversation moves on, meanders. Hera shares her next plan. Demeter expands on her love life, and Ananke offers to go shopping with her. You don't say much. You scowl and keep your head bowed. I've ruined your evening, haven't I?

Later, as everyone is preparing to leave, Aphrodite kisses your cheek and smiles politely at me. "Nyx, thank you for introducing us to your friend. It's been … a pleasure. See you next week?"

"Yes. Bye," You shepherd me away. I sense your annoyance. "I was trying to help you, you know," you say as we head for the exit.

You glance back. Everyone is still talking, their heads bent together, stealing glances in our direction. They're talking about me, but I don't care.

"There's nothing wrong with my life. I'm sorry if you need these … people …but I don't."

"Well, that went well."

You phone at half-seven, just as I'm shovelling muesli into my mouth, and I really don't want to talk to you. You've calmed down enough to talk pleasantly, but not warmly.

I wave to Husband as he leaves for work. He doesn't even pause for a kiss anymore.

"I don't get why you even took me." I dump my bowl in the sink, and grab my mug of tea. "I'm not completely sure why *you* go, to be honest."

You sigh. I know that sigh. "It gets lonely, being a single mum. I need something for me. I don't want another relationship, not yet—but I need *something*."

"You've got me."

"I've got you *sometimes*, when I can convince you that the house won't fall down without you."

"But ..."

"I just wish you'd given it more of a chance. You need that group as much as I do. When was the last time you did something for yourself, something completely wild?" You hang up before I answer, but it's not the last I'll hear about it.

I wake Son up, kicking his bed, and grab yesterday's discarded clothes from the floor. I distractedly pick up several empty crisp packets and throw them in his bin. I use one of his t-shirts to dust the banister on my way downstairs. I take a final mouthful of tepid tea, and rush out of the door.

There's a traffic jam, again. I listen to the same songs as yesterday on the radio. I drive the same roads, turn at the same junctions, stop at the same traffic lights.

You're right, I had dreams once. I had plans. This journey—this life—was not part of it.

I wanted a tattoo. I almost got one. Until I met Husband and he said he didn't like them.

I wanted to go back to university and do my Masters. Until I met Husband, and he wanted to start a family. He wanted to marry me, he said. I could study later, afterward, he *said*.

And now it's *afterward* and I haven't. I probably won't now. What's the point? I don't need a Masters to be a school secretary. Okay, so it's not the job I wanted, it's the one that fitted around my kids and Husband. But ...

Damn you. You've got me thinking, got me wondering what my life would have been like. I don't want to think about it, I don't want to know. I'm happy. I love my husband, and I love my kids. Why have you made me think I shouldn't?

I sit at my desk and type. I sit in a meeting and take minutes. I sit on reception and listen to the inane chatter of seven-year-olds.

I have a good life. What would I have done with my Masters anyway? How much would I have regretted that tattoo?

On the way home, I dig out the Queensryche CD hidden in the glove compartment. I want to listen to it, loudly, while I drive in a direction that isn't home. I shoved it in there ages ago when Husband sneered at it and asked for *something else.* So we listened to his music instead. I don't like his music any more than he likes Queensryche.

"Hey." I call home impulsively and Son answers. "I'm going to be late. Can you put the oven on? There's leftovers in the fridge. I'll be back by six."

"Uh, yeah." He grunts and hangs up.

I don't know what to do now. I don't remember the last time I had an hour to myself. I park up in the middle of town. A proliferation of hairdressers and charity shops has appeared since the last time I had time to just wander around. Normally, with kids or Husband in tow, I rush in and out as fast as possible. In the window of the CLIC shop, a mannequin wears an outrageous '70s outfit. I stare at it, wondering who could have possibly donated it.

How fantastic it would be to pop in and spend a tenner on clothes I never normally wear; how amazing it would be to show them off to Husband and watch his reaction.

Next door is a tattoo parlour. Again, I stand outside and stare. In the window are photos of newly-inked skin, looking red and swollen for the most part. Several tattoos are small and delicate, fitting neatly onto shoulders or wrists. A butterfly design catches my eye, vibrantly multi-coloured. I stare for so long, I don't see the guy inside watching me.

"All right, there?" he asks, peering out from the door.

"Yeah. Just looking."

"Is it your first?"

"Oh, I won't get one. I wanted to, a long time ago, but …"

"You should come in, have a proper look."

I'm tempted. I glance back at the window, at the beautiful butterflies, and shake my head. "I have to go," I say with a civil smile. "Maybe another time."

Next Wednesday, I'll follow you through that pub again. I'll stop off at the bar and buy two large white wines, one for you by way of an apology. When Aphrodite says, "Tell me about yourself," I'll have a better reply.

Bringing Back the Memories

You watch when I walk down the street; you all pause and turn. Silent and brazen. Sometimes there's a whisper, or a nudge between people. You're not subtle, none of you.

Strength in numbers, I guess. All of you against me, alone.

You watch while I struggle to walk, my balance not what it used to be. I have to live with this for the rest of my life. Not that you've thought about that. I'm just an easy target, the girl who crashed her car and killed her best friend.

Today, I've had enough. Today, it's time I told you my story, the *real* story. In my day-dreams, we're already sitting at a table, with coffees in front of us. We're already half-way through the conversation that will exonerate me. You nod, and realize that you've judged me severely.

Real life is different. I can't just accost you in the street and say, "It wasn't like that at all." You'd ask what *did* happen, what my *real* story is. But my blacked-out state prevents me from remembering. My brain-damaged speech prevents me from explaining. It would be a futile endeavour.

They said I'd been drinking, the police who watched me cut out of the wreckage. They checked the skid marks on the road and said I'd been speeding. But they're wrong. You are *all* wrong.

Aren't you?

I've stopped walking. I don't know how long I've been statuesque like this in the middle of the street, but my legs feel too heavy to continue. You're starting to gather around me like vultures. I'm scared of you.

I didn't stand trial. Once I got out of hospital, the extent of my injuries was clear. There was no way I could testify, no way I could be jailed, if found guilty. The local paper called it a disgrace. You all agreed. The whole town against me, and I couldn't defend myself. It's not enough that my body and mind are broken beyond repair.

The effort of moving again is too much. Putting one foot in front of the other takes a focus that I just don't have any more. You're walking around me, pushing past me, carrying on with your day while I struggle. I see you, you know. I see your eyes boring into me, burning me, pinning me down.

One day, the doctors said, my memory might return. They said it could happen gradually, a small piece of the puzzle fitting with all the others. Or it might be an attack, a sudden deluge of information. I dread the day I'll know the truth, the day when your stares and comments make sense.

Jump

You sit on the edge of the cliff, staring down at the rocks, at the sea swirling and crashing against them. The sun set an hour ago. Now the air all around you is inky. But you stare out as though you can still see the horizon.

You've lost count of the number of hours you've sat here, waiting.

Today.

Yesterday.

Last week.

I know—I've added them up. I've watched you waiting for him to come back, deep down knowing he won't. Deep down knowing he's lost down there, trapped in the wreckage. I've counted every hour, and been here beside you.

You take your phone from your pocket and dial your voicemail. You listen to his voice, his final message. It's nothing special—he wanted you to buy milk on your way home. You smile, knowing how much he hated leaving messages. Usually he texted, so he obviously expected you to answer the call. He *um'ed* for a moment, then hung up, without even saying goodbye.

That's it. That's all you have. He never even said goodbye.

You listen again, dejected. You look like you're going to talk to him, but in the end you drop the phone from your ear and listen to his voice floating out across the cliffs. *Get milk*, he tells you. You hate milk.

You glance down over the edge. I sense your fear and confusion, your disorientation as the sea swirls. You can't judge the distance—it seems like all you need to do is take just one step and you'll be swimming in the sea. Just one step, and you can be with him again.

With your growing desire to jump, I am increasingly corporeal, until I am a faint outline, although barely discernible to you.

I don't move, don't make myself known. I simply sit next to you and wait until the point you know you can't go on. I'll wait until you resolve that today's the day you're going to do it. I'll leave it until that final moment, that point beyond all doubt, and I'll take your arm and pull you back.

One Last Dance

Our family is all around us. Kids, grandkids, great grandkids. And so many friends. They surprised us with this party—we weren't planning to celebrate, under the circumstances, but I'm glad they did. You look so beautiful, just like the eighteen-year-old I married sixty years ago.

You're sitting at a table, clapping along to the music, bobbing your head and singing. You know all the words to whatever the hell this barrage is. Grandchildren were in charge of the entertainment; apparently, twenty-somethings have no idea what a proper tune sounds like.

"Katy Perry," you mouth across to me, exaggerating the words and repeating them until I understand. You could always read my mind, an endearing skill you utilize most frequently during arguments. You laugh at my bemusement. I'm not sure what I'd do without you to laugh at me.

"Gramps, dance with me." My hand is tugged and I look down, all the way down, to the youngest of my great-grandchildren, Emily, the little blondie. She jumps up and down on the end of my arm.

"Of course, milady." I bow gallantly, and we walk onto the dance floor.

It's not so easy, these days—my legs are stiff and sore, my hips crack loudly. None of that bothers Emily, though, she just twists around, holding both of my hands, and doesn't seem to notice that I'm not moving so much.

You watch me, with that special smile, the one that makes you look like Audrey Hepburn, the one that only *I* see. And immediately I want to dance with you. I want to hold you in my arms and swirl you around like I used to. It's been a long time—too long. You used to love dancing, used to love going out. You could spend hours getting ready, so that your dress and hair and makeup were just so, and we'd stay on our feet all night, barely pausing for a drink.

I bow to Emily once again, and walk over to you. "May I have this dance, Miss?"

"Oh, darling, you know … you know I can't." You shake your head and frown. I didn't mean to upset you. I want to give you a memory that will last forever.

"Sssh." I hold your hand, and with Aiden's help, I pull you to your feet.

You reach for your walking sticks and take a step or two. I cover your hand with mine, and you understand my intention. You release your sticks and allow me to take them from you.

"I've got you." I catch your weight. I'm weaker than I expected, but you're so slight now, I can still hold you.

We walk to the dance floor. Aiden walks alongside us, his hands ready to catch us should one of us fall. I wish we didn't need him, but I'm grateful.

People are watching us, turning and nudging others until the whole room is turned to us. They applaud when our song starts to play. They shed tears when you rest your head on my shoulder. They take video or photos, catching the moment, to remember.

You are still the most beautiful woman I have ever seen, and I still can't believe I have spent these past sixty years with you. I dip my head, smell your perfume, and feel your body moving slowly beside mine.

This might be our last dance, and I want to remember every single detail.

Watching the Storms Roll In

We sit on the beach, you and I, side by side. I've taken off my shoes and burrowed my feet into the sand. We watch the storm coming in, the bubbling black clouds and the faint growl of thunder.

"We should go, before the rain comes," you say, although neither of us moves.

You wrap your arm around me, but I shrug you away. Immediately, I regret it—you look so forlorn and uncertain.

"It's not …" I try to explain, but my words dissolve. "I just …"

Actually, I have no idea why I did that. I watch you for a moment, then stare down at my feet in the sand, digging further in.

You're my first boyfriend. I have nothing to compare you to. Sometimes, I wonder whether I should love you more, or if I would love someone else more. How do you know?

In our silence, the waves become louder, crashing over the rocks at the base of the cliff, splashing onto the shore. It's the noise of my childhood, the soundtrack of my life. I sway in time with the ebb and flow.

"Marry me?" you say, producing a ring from goodness knows where. It's stunning, a small diamond, understated and elegant. It never occurred to me, when you were questioning my tastes, that this is what you had in mind.

"Yes. Oh, yes!"

It's a perfect fit. I stare at my finger, tilting my hand back and forth to catch the diamond in the glow of the restaurant lights. It's so surreal. I snuggle into you and let myself sink into your arms. I see our life together, our perfect life, stretching out.

I lift my head slightly so I can watch you. I love the tuft of chest hair that peeks out of your shirt, the uneven stubble on your jaw. I love the wink you give me when you notice me looking, and I blush. Even now, after more than a year together, you still make me blush. I love you.

You reach down to kiss the top of my head. I love the warmth of your breath.

Heavy rain clouds thicken, blurring the horizon, creeping towards us. And, still, I don't want to go home. I want to be here with you, always.

Around us, other people aren't so hardy. They pack up their picnic bags, dry off their children, gather bats and balls and buckets and spades. A family pause in front of us. "Hey, are you okay? Do you need help back to the top?"

There are one hundred and thirty-three steps to the top of the cliff. Holidaymakers can usually be found hanging around the half-way mark—checking out the view, they explain, as us locals dash past.

I shake my head with a smile. "No, we're fine, thanks. I think we're going to stay a little longer."

"Not too much longer, I hope. That storm's coming in fast."

"Oh, I like the rain."

The man glances at his wife and they share the kind of indecipherable couple's look that we often share. The wife knows exactly what her husband is thinking, but I can only assume.

"Well, okay, if you're sure …" and they walk away, without even a goodbye.

I watch them sludge through the soft sand, past the bar and the wooden hut that serves as the shop. They pause when they reach the concrete platform and stare up at the cliff, mentally preparing themselves for those one hundred and thirty-three steps.

"That was weird," I say, turning back to you. "Why did they think we needed help?"

"I have no idea."

I glance down and realize my bump is protruding, looking much bigger in my billowing top than I'd hoped. "The baby's kicking. Do you want to feel?"

I position your hand in the optimum place and wait. When the baby kicks you exclaim, and the look on your face is a mixture of pride and amazement and fear. You wait for more, and each time, you make that same squealing sound. I cover your hand with mine.

"Watch this." I push down, and the baby pushes back. I push down twice, and the baby responds in kind.

"He's really real," you say with a tear in your eye.

"You want a boy?"

"I don't really mind, as long as it's healthy, but I imagine a boy."

"We should start thinking about names."

"Christopher," you say without missing a beat, and I know you're thinking of your baby brother who died when you were so young.

I nod. "And Daisy, for a girl."

A flash of lightning spreads across the sky. I duck and you laugh. We count the seconds out loud. Twelve seconds until the thunder reverberates. "Twelve miles," you say.

"We don't have to go yet, do we?" It's not raining, and the heat is intense and sticky. I don't want to go home and be enclosed by walls.

"We should get Daisy to bed soon." You look at your watch. I look at the child dozing in my arms. "It's almost six."

"She's fine. Fast asleep. I just want to watch the storm a bit longer."

"She might get scared."

"My daughter isn't scared of anything." And I bend down to kiss her clammy forehead. You reach out to stroke her soft hair.

How is it possible we can love this little person so much when we've known her for such a short time?

A helicopter flies directly over us. I follow it across the sky, captivated. Flying always amazes me—it's so completely unnaturally impossible. I've often wondered how those Wright brothers took such a daft idea and made it real. But then, I wonder the same about telephones and televisions. I don't tell people that.

"There's probably been an accident," I say.

"No, they're circling back. I think it's a search party." We watch it arc around and come back towards us.

"How awful." I'm glad you're here with me, not missing, not lost.

Three flashes of lightning brighten the sky in quick succession, giving shape to the mass of clouds and making the dark cliffs look as though they're falling down upon us.

I reach out to hold your hand, but you seem further away now. I wasn't conscious of you moving. You're staring down at the sand, sweeping your fingers through it, making shapes.

Daisy stirs in my arms. She thrusts her fist into her mouth and chews, making soft little sighs. I rock her backward and forward until she's calm and quiet again.

"What's wrong?"

You say nothing, and I feel tears pricking my eyes. I don't understand. I don't remember arguing with you, but you're solid, unyielding. Your arms are folded and hostile. I hate to feel unloved by you. I am broken without you.

"Talk to me," I demand, but you barely look at me. I ought to sidle across to you, to wrap my arms around you, but something stops me. I hold Daisy close and imagine her growing up without you. "Please."

It's the catch in my voice that causes you to glance up. You're silent and still for a while, then I see your own tears. I smile coyly and, eventually, you wink. You shuffle toward me, a little at a time, until you're beside me again, back where you belong. Nothing keeps us apart, you and I, always together.

"I—I forgot to tell you, I got offered that promotion," you say after a while, like it's no big deal.

"That's fantastic, well done!" You've worked hard for it, diligently. You deserve it.

"I was thinking we could move, get somewhere bigger, so Daisy won't have to share her room with the new baby."

The bump kicks into my ribs. "He likes that."

"Oh, it's a he, is it?" you tease.

"Well, I was right about Daisy being a girl, wasn't I? A mother knows …" I tap the side of my nose with my finger. It's a trait from my own mother, and I groan with the realization— you feign horror that I'm turning into her.

"Mummy, look at me," Daisy calls from the edge of the water. She's jumping over the waves as they roll in.

"Be careful, don't fall," I call back.

A wave splashes over her. She screams and runs back toward us. She stumbles on the soft sand, and she's crying now, wiping sandy/salty hands across her face. You run to her, bend down and wipe her eyes. You sweep her up and she wraps her arms around your neck. You're her hero as well as mine. Mine and Christopher's, I correct myself, staring down at the soft baby blue eyes that are fixed on me. He stops suckling for a moment, and even though it's far too early, I swear he smiles.

"We're so lucky, you and Daisy and I, because Daddy loves us so much."

The air crackles with electricity, muggy and oppressive. My blouse clings to my back. I long to feel cool rain on my skin. I consider paddling in the sea, but the waves are becoming more ferocious and would probably sweep me off my feet.

The thunder and lightning edges closer. We watch a bolt hit

the headland, and all say *ooh* in unison, like we're watching fireworks, which makes us laugh. Five seconds, this time, between the bright flash and the long drawn out rumble echoing around the bay.

That helicopter passes over again. I feel sorry for whoever is lost out there tonight, for their family waiting anxiously for news. I feel guilty that I'm sharing tonight with my family, while somewhere on the cliffs, or out at sea, someone is all alone.

"Are you okay?" you ask, full of concern.

"I was just thinking how lucky I am."

I watch the kids making sandcastles. One, two, three bucket shaped towers all in a row. Daisy is ordering her brother to do this or that, to dig the moat, to fetch seaweed and shells. But Christopher's too little to understand properly and he's just flinging sand around with his spade.

A flash, a roar: one second. The storm is almost directly upon us, and yet there's still no rain. It'll pour down soon, cascading from the sky as though someone has turned on a tap. You'll tell me we have to go, again, in a minute. But I really don't want to. I'm happy here. I've always been happy here.

"Time passes so quickly, doesn't it?" I say almost to myself, gazing out at the empty beach. Daisy and Christopher are just ghosts here now, teenagers with their own lives, not wanting to even be seen with us anymore. I lean into you and feel the warmth of your torso. I didn't realize I was getting so cold, but now I start to shiver.

"We should get you home," you say as, finally, the first drop falls on us, and the torrent unleashes. We're soaked through immediately. I shriek and you laugh, and I wish we could be happy like this forever.

I gasp as the lightning splits off into three or four forks. I jump at the crash of thunder. You stand up and brush sand off your legs. In the darkness, I can barely see your face—you're all in shadow.

"Mum? Mum?"

I look around. Christopher and his wife are tripping over the sand towards me. Behind them are two police officers. Their torches shine into our eyes and we're startled rabbits, you and I.

"We've been looking everywhere for you," Christopher says, kneeling beside me and hugging me, both arms wrapped tightly around me, his chin resting on the top of my head. "You shouldn't wander off like that. You scared the hell out of us," He takes a deep breath. "You scared me."

"I was perfectly safe. I was with your father. We were watching the storm." I turn to you for corroboration, but you're not there.

I can still feel your hands on my shoulder, but you're not here.

"Oh Mum." Christopher's shoulders slump and he shakes his head. "We can't go on like this," he says to no one in particular. He stands up and looks down at me, just the way you used to when you were exasperated or disappointed with me. It wasn't often, of course, but sometimes ...

It's Amy and one of the policemen who help me to my feet. My hips ache from sitting in the same position for so long. My knees creak. I smooth my dress across my thighs, and glance back to where we were sitting, you and I. Christopher takes my arm, and I hobble alongside him to the base of the cliff. I wonder how I'll manage all those steps without you.

Acknowledgements

With thanks to the elderly couple eating their lunch at the garden centre.

With thanks to my 14-year-old self who plastered her wall with posters.

With thanks to my sons, my husband and the family members who give me such great inspiration.

With thanks to Kyra Lennon for throwing out the weak links in this collection with a big red NO.

With thanks to my sofa in front of my bedroom window.

With thanks to The Liscawn beer garden, and the gorgeous cider they provided while I wrote two of these stories.

With thanks to my grandmother who explained the importance of opening windows.

With thanks to the judges and organizers of the Costa Short Story Award 2015, and the members of the public who voted *Watching The Storms Roll In* to 3rd Place.

With thanks to everyone at Vine Leaves Press for believing in this collection.

Vine Leaves Press

Enjoyed this book?
Go to *vineleavespress.com* to find more.

Lightning Source UK Ltd.
Milton Keynes UK
UKOW02f1055010516

273314UK00001B/1/P